Warning Shot

Slocum opened his fist and let Lem's head fall forward. He kept the Colt aimed at the man as he stood up and dusted himself off a bit. "I meant to deliver this message to you in a more civil manner, but you forced the issue by lurking in alleyways and shooting through windows. Eliza Banner is to be left alone. Deliver that message to whoever hired you because if I have to send another one, it won't be so nice."

Pulling himself up, Lem said, "Oh, I will. You wanna tell me who the hell you are? That way we'll know what to write on yer grave marker."

Slocum turned, aimed, and fired in one smooth motion. The Colt Navy barked once and sent its bullet into the ground between Lem's fingers. "I'm the man that'll be keeping an eye on Miss Banner. That's all you need to know."

JAKE LOGAN

SLOCUM
AND
THE LUCKY LADY

J

JOVE BOOKS, NEW YORK

THE BERKLEY PUBLISHING GROUP
Published by the Penguin Group
Penguin Group (USA) Inc.
375 Hudson Street, New York, New York 10014, USA
Penguin Group (Canada), 90 Eglinton Avenue East, Suite 700, Toronto, Ontario M4P 2Y3, Canada
(a division of Pearson Penguin Canada Inc.)
Penguin Books Ltd., 80 Strand, London WC2R 0RL, England
Penguin Group Ireland, 25 St. Stephen's Green, Dublin 2, Ireland (a division of Penguin Books Ltd.)
Penguin Group (Australia), 250 Camberwell Road, Camberwell, Victoria 3124, Australia
(a division of Pearson Australia Group Pty. Ltd.)
Penguin Books India Pvt. Ltd., 11 Community Centre, Panchsheel Park, New Delhi—110 017, India
Penguin Group (NZ), 67 Apollo Drive, Rosedale, North Shore 0632, New Zealand
(a division of Pearson New Zealand Ltd.)
Penguin Books (South Africa) (Pty.) Ltd., 24 Sturdee Avenue, Rosebank, Johannesburg 2196,
South Africa

Penguin Books Ltd., Registered Offices: 80 Strand, London WC2R 0RL, England

This is a work of fiction. Names, characters, places, and incidents either are the product of the author's imagination or are used fictitiously, and any resemblance to actual persons, living or dead, business establishments, events, or locales is entirely coincidental.

SLOCUM AND THE LUCKY LADY

A Jove Book / published by arrangement with the author

PRINTING HISTORY
Jove edition / March 2009

Copyright © 2009 by Penguin Group (USA) Inc.
Cover illustration by Sergio Giovine.

ISBN: 978-0-515-14594-6

JOVE®
Jove Books are published by The Berkley Publishing Group,
a division of Penguin Group (USA) Inc.
375 Hudson Street, New York, New York 10014.
JOVE® is a registered trademark of Penguin Group (USA) Inc.
The "J" design is a trademark of Penguin Group (USA) Inc.

PRINTED IN THE UNITED STATES OF AMERICA

10 9 8 7 6 5 4 3 2 1

1

There wasn't much in the town of East Padre to hold anyone's attention for long. Situated on the easternmost border
of New Mexico, the town was a collection of dusty shacks
and a few leaning structures that had been built up enough to
support a second floor. When the wind blew, every one of
those buildings creaked loudly enough to be heard all the
way to West Texas.

East Padre had a few saloons, a billiard room, and more
than enough whores to wander through them all. There were
a couple stores and even a blacksmith, but those places looked
to be struggling for customers in a town where most folks
were only passing through before heading east into Texas or
north into the mountains. Greener pastures lay to the west as
well but, compared to what East Padre had to offer, any pas-
ture was greener.

It was late in the day and the sun was dipping below the
western horizon. Once the general store was locked up, East
Padre was handed over to the drunks and rowdies who stag-
gered in and out of the establishments that catered to their
needs. An occasional shot rang out, but that was nothing new.
The locals standing along the streets or gazing out their windows didn't even flinch at gunfire. They simply cast their eyes

about and looked to see if the town's sorry excuse for a law-man would actually take the time to check on the matter. When neither the lawman nor either of his two deputies both-ered to show, those meandering eyes simply turned in another direction. If someone was shot, there wasn't much to do about it anyhow. The closest doctor was six miles away and any poor bastard who caught a bullet would surely die before he got so much as a stitch. If the patient lived, the wound wasn't bad enough to warrant a fuss.

Another shot cut through the air, but still didn't catch much attention. The thunder of hooves beat against the ground, accompanied by the sound of voices shouting back and forth between nearly half a dozen men. A few curious locals wan-dered outside to crane their necks and swap guesses as to where all the ruckus was coming from. Judging by the point-ing fingers and waving hands, the consensus was somewhere down along Second Street. This was no surprise, since it was a rare occasion when shots weren't fired from one of the rowdy houses along Second Street.

The locals shrugged to themselves and got back to their own business. The ones who still had some walking to do put their heads down and made sure to steer clear of Second Street.

Another shot was fired. This time, the bullet whipped across Second Street and buried itself into the wall of the Crippled Mule Saloon just below the roofline and just above one of the windows on the second floor. It was one of the few places in town to have a second floor, serve hot grub, and pour fairly good whiskey to wash it down. Those things were enough to hold John Slocum's interest.

Slocum hadn't intended on staying in town for longer than it took to catch his breath and wash the dirt from his face. But after he broke up a fight in the saloon, the barkeep offered to pay him back with a few free meals, free drinks, and a room on the second floor. If Slocum hadn't been so hungry after eating a steady diet of beans and jerky on the trail, he might have tipped his hat and refused the offer. But sometimes things tended to taste better when they were free.

The Crippled Mule also had something else that set the place aside from the other saloons in town: a little blonde named Alice. She served drinks in the saloon, and had been batting her eyelashes at Slocum after she'd seen him toss those angry drunks on their asses a few nights ago. Since then, she'd taken it upon herself to deliver Slocum's whiskey directly up to his room. He guessed he wasn't the first to receive such service, but he was pretty sure he was the only one getting the deliveries over the last few nights. Slocum had been keeping Alice too occupied for her to make the rounds anywhere else.

When the nearby gunshot went off across the street, Slocum was too busy to notice.

When that bullet punched through the wall only a few feet over his head, the loud crack was more than enough to catch his attention.

"What the hell was that?" Slocum asked as he looked up toward the splintered wooden planks.

Alice was on her knees in front of him, grabbing Slocum's hips in both hands and pulling herself forward while sliding her lips along the length of his cock. Her dark blond hair came down just past her shoulders, where it spilled along her naked skin and stopped short at the slope of her breasts. The top of her dress was unbuttoned and peeled down to expose her from the waist up. When she leaned back and let Slocum fall out of her mouth, Alice squinted and angled her face toward the window.

"What was what?" she asked.

"That gunshot. Didn't you hear it?"

Alice chuckled and stroked his cock to keep it hard. "There's always gunshots this time of night. Ain't you ever heard them before?"

"This one was close, though," Slocum said. "A mite too close for my liking."

"Then I'd best keep my head down." With that, Alice slid

her hands down along Slocum's legs and wrapped her lips once more around the tip of his rigid pole. Her lips were full and she slid them expertly along his length. As she did, she pressed her tongue against the underside of his penis and teased him all the way down to its base.

As much as Slocum wanted to stay out of the path of another bullet, it was difficult for him to take his mind away from the touch of Alice's tongue against his skin. Also, she was right. Gunshots weren't exactly rare at this time of night. He reached down for her, intending to ease her head back so he could get to the gun belt slung across the back of a nearby chair. The moment his fingers slipped through her hair, however, Alice let out a contented moan that Slocum could feel all the way down to his feet.

Alice leaned forward and took every inch of him into her mouth. Once she had him engulfed, she stayed put and kept moaning softly from the back of her throat.

Slocum pushed Alice back, but only to keep from finishing right then and there. "All right," he said. "You may not be worried about a bit of gunfire, but I don't intend on getting shot for standing in the wrong place at the wrong time."

Smirking as she dabbed at the corners of her mouth, Alice stood up and turned so her back was against the wall next to the window. She was a short little thing, but had more than enough curves to fill out her petite frame. Large breasts, capped with pink nipples the size of silver dollars, swayed invitingly as she situated her shoulders against the splintered wooden window frame.

Although Slocum meant to study the street in front of the saloon for any trace of the owlhoots who'd fired the shots at his window, his eyes were soon drawn to another sight. Alice gazed over at him, keeping her back arched and her shoulders pressed against the wall. Tracing one hand between her breasts, she reached out with the other to tug on the front of Slocum's unbuttoned shirt.

"You want to keep lookin' out that window?" Alice asked. "Or do you want to keep lookin' at me?"

There were a few people in the street, but the sight of them wasn't nearly as interesting as the show Alice was currently putting on. Still pulling Slocum closer, she'd moved her other hand down until she could hook her thumb beneath the material of her dress that had been rolled down to her waist. From there, Alice pushed the material down even further to expose the smooth skin of her belly. A little lower, and the dress was down far enough to give Slocum a peek at the thatch of hair between her legs.

Even as Slocum turned away from the window, his body was already reacting to the sight of Alice's body. His cock was rock hard by the time he roughly pulled Alice's dress the rest of the way down over her wide hips. Her generous curves were outlined by the pale light drifting in through the window, and the way she arched her back made her plump breasts stand out even more.

Now it was Slocum's turn to grab her hips. Having already felt her respond to a bit of roughness before, he grabbed her ass and pulled her close enough to feel his erection against her body.

"That's it, John," she groaned. "That's just how I like it."

Slocum knew that well enough already. Rather than carry her over to the bed where they'd tussled so many times already, he lifted her up, carried her to a spot away from the window, and pinned her against the wall. Alice reacted quickly by wrapping her arms around the back of his neck and her legs around his waist.

"I thought you were worried about those shots," Alice teased as her eyes widened.

Shifting his hips until he felt his cock slide between the wet lips of Alice's pussy, Slocum tightened his grip on her ass and pulled her closer while easing his rigid member inside. "Maybe I've got better things on my mind right now," he told her.

Alice closed her eyes and let out a breathy moan. "I can feel that much."

Slocum pumped his hips between her legs. His hands

grabbed hold of her ample backside to keep her in place as he continued to thrust in a slow, powerful rhythm.

Every time he buried himself in her, Alice dug her fingernails into Slocum's shoulders. Even as a few more gunshots were fired outside, she only responded to the motion of Slocum's body between her thighs and the hardness that was sliding in and out of her.

Slocum could hear the gunshots. He just didn't give a damn about them anymore now that he was distracted by the touch of Alice's large breasts against his bare chest. He could feel her nipples growing hard as her muscles began to twitch beneath her skin. Judging by Alice's loud moans along with that trembling, she was getting close to a climax. Slocum could feel her pussy tightening around him more and more, so he quickened his pace to drive her over the edge.

He didn't have to work for long before Alice cinched her legs and arms around him even tighter. Her eyes were clamped shut and her hips bucked against him until she barely had enough strength to hold her head up.

Now that she wasn't bucking and squirming so much, Slocum could hold her where he wanted so he could enter her just right. It was amazing what a slightly different angle could do, and he felt the difference as soon as he pulled her hips away from the wall so her upper body was leaning slightly away from him. From there, he could resume pumping in and out of her while enjoying the view of her naked body.

Still reveling in her own pleasure, Alice kept her eyes closed and grunted in approval every time Slocum buried himself all the way into her. Her nipples were standing at attention and her breasts swayed every time her shoulders hit the wall.

"Oh God, John," she moaned. "Oh . . . God!"

Just as Slocum felt his own fires rising in him, he could tell that Alice was about to burn up again as well. All he needed to do was grab hold of her and thrust his own hips forward to push both of them over the brink. Slocum leaned his head back and exploded inside her as Alice trembled and shook against him. Even after he was spent, Slocum was kept hard by the tight wet lips that were still wrapped around his cock.

"Damn," Alice breathed. "I hope some more of those assholes take a shot at this place."

Slocum leaned over so he could get another look out the window. As he lowered Alice to the floor, she got her legs beneath herself so she could stand up on her own. Alice was too short to keep him inside her once she was on her own two feet, so she took his penis in her hands and rubbed as if she was slowly trying to start a fire.

"What's outside that's so damned interesting?" she asked.

"Looks like there's trouble," Slocum replied.

"There's always trouble of some sort. How about I take your mind off of it for a bit longer?" Cupping him in one hand, she eased herself down to her knees and then began licking him. Her tongue darted along his length as if she was savoring the taste of her own juices as much as she was enjoying the taste of him.

Before Slocum could give himself over to what she was doing to him, he was distracted by a sudden stomping noise. "Did you hear footsteps outside?"

Alice chuckled and rubbed him some more. "Not hardly. I doubt I could even hear a runaway stagecoach from in here right now."

"Not from the street," Slocum said. "From the hall. Right outside the door."

Before Alice could dismiss that notion as she had the first, there was a rattling followed by stomping just outside the door to Slocum's room.

"There," Slocum said. "That's what I heard."

As Slocum turned toward the door, he felt Alice tighten her grip on him.

"Stay here," she whined. "Whoever it is will move along and I'm sure them gunshots weren't anything to do with you."

Slocum made his way to the chair where his gun belt was hung. He took the Colt Navy from its holster and had his thumb on the hammer before he was close enough to reach for the door's handle. "I can't be so certain about that. Hand me my britches."

Alice might have playfully refused on any other night, but the gun in Slocum's hand made her think twice. The stomping in the hallway had gotten louder until it exploded into what sounded more like a stampede making its way through the second floor of the saloon. The expression on Alice's face had gone from playfulness to disappointment before finally settling upon fear as she reached out to the clothes that had been piled up against the wall. After tossing Slocum his pants, she gathered up the dress that he'd all but ripped off of her.

Slocum got one leg into his britches and then jumped away from the door as something heavy smashed against the other side of it. The back of Slocum's legs knocked against the rickety frame of his bed, causing him to drop onto the mattress. Even as he lost his balance and fell onto the bed, Slocum managed to raise his gun to aim at the door.

Old wood cracked against the heel of a well-placed boot, sending the door smashing inward to smack against the wall. The man who'd done the kicking was big enough to fill up the doorway and then some. He was built more solidly than the rest of the saloon and had a full, brushy beard covering the better portion of his face. Once the door was out of his way, he took one step into the room and found himself staring down the business end of Slocum's Colt.

"State your business and be damn quick about it," Slocum growled.

Under normal circumstances, it might have seemed appropriate for a man to laugh after stumbling into a room to find another fellow standing there holding a tussled pair of jeans up to cover himself. In this circumstance, however, the man holding the jeans was also holding a pistol, and that didn't strike the big man in the doorway as funny in the least.

Shifting his eyes to look past Slocum, the bearded man grunted, "Who's that?"

"I'm the one with the gun, mister," Slocum warned. "So I'm the one making demands." Thumbing back the Colt's hammer, he added, "State your business or get out of my room before I hollow out that oversized head of yours."

If the bearded man was frightened at the prospect of being in Slocum's sights, he didn't let on. Instead, he craned his neck to get a look at Alice. His mouth hung open to reveal several spaces between the crooked, grimy teeth that remained in his head. The big man let out a breath that stank of bad cheese and looked at Slocum's pistol. Letting his eyes take in the rest of the sights, he grunted, "You should put some clothes on, mister."

"I'd just have to wash them after I blow your brains all over this room."

"Fine, fine. I'm leavin'," the big man said. "That ain't the bitch we was after anyhow."

"Hey!" Alice snapped. "What did you call me?"

The big man smirked as he backed out to the hall and then turned to walk toward the stairs that led down to the saloon's main floor. Slocum kept his gun aimed at the man's back as he leaned out to watch him stomp down the stairs. Just as he was about to step back into his room, the door across from him was flung open and another pair of gunmen stormed outside.

The one to walk out first wore a battered brown hat that cast a shadow over a rough, scarred face. "What the hell you lookin' at?" he asked as he turned to stomp toward the stairs.

The second gunman was a skinny fellow with long hair and small round spectacles perched on his nose. He didn't have any threats or insults to throw in Slocum's direction, but he did have a shotgun pointed at Slocum's doorway.

Slocum reacted before he could think about it. Despite the fact that he was already holding his gun, he knew he wouldn't be able to take his shot before that shotgun went off. He also had recognized the cold look in the skinny fellow's eyes that told him the shotgun would most definitely be going off sooner rather than later. After all of that blazed through Slocum's mind, he leaned toward the bed and pushed himself away from the doorway using both feet.

The shotgun roared, filling the hallway with smoke and Slocum's room with flying lead. Before his chest hit the mattress, Slocum felt something rake across his hip like a set of eagle's talons. He skidded along the top of the bed and tucked his head in close to his chest before dropping off the other side. Hitting the floor on his shoulder, Slocum growled an obscenity and looked around for Alice.

She was curled up in a ball less than a foot away from him.

"What's going on here?" she cried. "Who the hell are those men?"

After taking a quick look at the door, Slocum got to his feet and prepared himself to fire the gun in his hand. The pair that had come out of the room across the hall was already gone. By the sounds coming from the hallway, those two were on the heels of the big fellow who'd stomped down the stairs. "I was just about to ask you that same question," Slocum said as he quickly pulled on his pants.

"Maybe they're robbing the place!" Alice offered.

Touching the bloody spots on his hip to find only a few deep scratches, he said, "They were after someone."

"Who?"

"That's what I intend on finding out."

2

Even though Slocum was dressed when he came out of his room, he still looked as if he'd fallen off the back of a wagon. His shirt was crookedly buttoned and hanging over the top of his jeans. His boots had been hastily pulled over his feet and his hat was somewhere on the floor of his room. When he stomped into the hall, he wasn't looking for compliments on his appearance. He had a gun in his hand and was ready to use it. Judging by the commotion coming from the first floor, it wouldn't be long before he got his chance.

The main floor of the saloon looked as though it had been hit by a twister. Tables and chairs were scattered every which way. People were rushing to and fro. Punches were being thrown. A few pistols were skinned. All in all, it was business as usual for a busy night at the Crippled Mule. Since there was nothing unusual in all that, Slocum shoved through the crowd and went over to the stout fellow tending the bar.

"What can I do for ya, Mr. Slocum?" the barkeep asked.

"You can start by telling me where those assholes went after kicking in my door!"

"The who that did what?"

Reaching across the bar to grab hold of the stout man by

11

the front of his shirt, Slocum pulled the bartender closer and snarled at him through gritted teeth. "Three men just walked down those stairs. One kicked in my door and another fired a shotgun at me. Where the hell did they go?"

"I heard some shots, but I thought there was just a dispute. I didn't know—"

"Tell me where they went!"

"The three that came downstairs walked straight out the front door," the barkeep replied. "I was glad to see 'em go."

Slocum released the barkeep's shirt and turned toward the door.

"I wouldn't go after them just yet," the bartender warned. "They seemed awfully upset about something or other."

"That makes two of us."

Not eager to get in Slocum's way, the barkeep raised his hands and stepped back. After Slocum had left, the barkeep tried to regain his composure by chuckling and straightening the front of his shirt. "It ain't nothing," he said to one of the nearby drunks. "We're just fooling. Need another bottle?"

Outside, Slocum prepared himself for anything. He'd been looking for any of those three men, or any number of rowdies that meant to meet up with them outside. He'd even expected to be fired upon as soon as he showed his face outside the saloon. In fact, Slocum had been hoping someone was foolish enough to present themselves as an easy target while the fire was still hot in Slocum's belly.

But the only folks Slocum saw directly outside the saloon were gaping back at him as if they were more afraid of him than anything else. Holstering the Colt, Slocum took a few steps forward so he could look up and down the street. Less than half the torches along the street were lit, making it difficult for him to see much of anything.

"You looking for the three that charged out of there?"

Turning toward the person who'd spoken up, Slocum found an old-timer sitting with his back propped up against the side of a watering trough. "I sure am," Slocum said.

"Then you'll want to go thataway," the old-timer said as he swung an arm toward the north end of Second Street.

Since he didn't have any better ideas of his own, Slocum followed the vagrant's advice and took off in that direction. In the state of mind he was in, Slocum would have been just as happy to walk into an ambush as he would have been to find the three gunmen sitting on a porch swing waiting for him. Either way, he'd be able to give those assholes a piece of his mind.

Slocum made it to the corner and glanced to his left and right. The three men were easy enough to spot, since they were walking shoulder to shoulder with their guns drawn. Grinning as he ducked into the shadows beneath the awning connecting a short row of shops, Slocum hurried to close the distance between himself and the trio of gunmen. Once he'd gotten to well within pistol range and was fairly certain there was nobody else around him, Slocum planted his feet on the sorry excuse for a boardwalk and rested his hand upon the ebony grip of his Colt and hollered, "What's the matter? You boys looking for another door to kick in?"

The first gunman to turn and face Slocum was the one who'd been with the long-haired fellow with the shotgun back at the Crippled Mule. Sharp eyes fixed on Slocum right away, but he kept his gun pointed at the street instead of taking up a fighting stance.

The skinny fellow with the long hair, glasses, and shotgun was just as quick to start something as he was when he'd been outside Slocum's room. He raised his shotgun, and was about to fire before his partner reached out to push the twin barrels down.

"Are you blind?" the first gunman asked. "That ain't who we're after!"

"Get yer hand off'a my gun, Mark," the skinny fellow growled. "He's comin' after us!"

The third gunman was actually the one who'd kicked in Slocum's door. The burly man with the shaggy beard stepped forward and waved away the other two as if he was silencing a pair of yelping kids. "If this man went through the trouble of comin' after us, maybe he's got somethin' on his mind."

"I sure as hell do," Slocum said. "I'd like to know why you busted into my room and fired a shotgun at me."

Upon hearing that last part, the burly man threw a sideways glance toward the fellow wearing the spectacles. The skinny man rolled his eyes and shrugged his shoulders. Looking back to Slocum, the big man said, "Honest mistake. You wanna make somethin' of it or you wanna go back to the Mule and forget about it?"

After all the running about, Slocum had worked himself into a lather. Now that he'd had a chance to cool his heels, he let out a breath and reined himself in a bit. "Who were you after?"

"Someone named Banner."

"Can't think of anyone by that name."

"Then we can part ways," the big man said.

"Part ways so you can kick in more doors and fire that shotgun at a few more folks that were just going about their business?" Slocum asked. "I don't think so."

The gunman who the skinny fellow had called Mark narrowed his eyes and took a closer look at Slocum. "I don't see a badge on you, mister. You the law around here?"

"No."

"Then what business is it of yours what we do or where we go?"

As Slocum stood there and allowed his anger to simmer down, he could sense something else boiling around the three men. They were desperate to find whoever they were after. While Slocum wasn't the sort of man to take advantage of desperate folks, these three hadn't exactly proven themselves to be worthy of such consideration. Besides, Slocum's pockets were a bit empty and he could sniff out a good chance when he saw one.

"I'm not the law," Slocum said. "And I suppose our first meeting could be a simple mistake."

"That's mighty generous of you," the burly man said as he turned and gave one of his dismissive waves to Slocum.

"Now that we're talking like civilized folks," Slocum continued, "maybe we could discuss a matter of business."

Although the burly man was content to keep walking in the other direction, Mark held his ground and stared at Slocum like a dog trying to make sense of a bug flitting around his nose. Cocking his head slightly and scowling a bit, Mark asked, "What sort of business?"

"I've spent a lot of time at the Crippled Mule," Slocum replied. "I got a knack for remembering faces. If you're looking for someone who's supposed to be there, perhaps I could help."

"You said you ain't heard of anyone named Banner," the burly man pointed out.

"True enough, but I don't know everyone's name. Tell me who Banner is and I might have spotted him. I'm also a fair hand at tracking down people that don't want to be found. Considering how you men were going through that saloon, my guess is that this Banner fella has done something pretty bad to rile you all up."

"You got that right," the man with the long hair and spectacles said. "Banner owes us a whole lot of money and is hidin' somewhere in this shit-hole town." Furrowing his brow and raising his shotgun to aim at Slocum, he added, "Banner's also the sort to hire someone to cover his ass. Since you're the only one to come after us, maybe you're the one that was hired on."

Mark seemed to sense a storm was brewing because he suddenly shifted all of his focus toward the skinny man standing beside him. "Put that shotgun down, Lem! You damn near ruined everything back at that saloon."

Lem shifted his eyes toward Mark, but kept his shotgun aimed at Slocum. The muscles in his jaw tensed and he said, "You can't give me no orders. Besides, I didn't ruin anything!"

"You could'a killed someone back there," the big man snarled.

Compared to when Mark had scolded him, Lem seemed downright sheepish now that he was in the big man's sights. "Wasn't that the idea?"

"No!" Mark snapped. "The idea was to kill Banner. You're fixin' to either get us killed or hung by going off half-cocked the way you do."

Even from where he was standing, Slocum could see Lem's eyes twitching behind the glass of the skinny man's spectacles. The argument wasn't what Slocum had been after at the start, but he had to admit it was a hell of a show. Just to stoke the fire a bit, Slocum said, "I wouldn't be surprised if whoever you were after had enough time to settle into a good spot to pick all three of you off or just ride away in another direction."

The big man let out a slow breath that built up to a rumbling sigh. He looked around and bared the few rotten teeth that were still in his mouth. "He's right, goddammit."

"What?" Mark snapped. "He don't even know what he's talking about!"

"Lem made enough noise to let him know we was comin', and the both of you have been wasting enough time to let a lame dog crawl away from us. Last time I checked, Banner had two good legs, so he could be all the way to Old Mexico by now."

"To hell with you, Dawes!" Lem shouted. He tightened his grip around his shotgun and then turned it so the barrel was pointing at the burly man.

Dawes scowled beneath the thick beard covering his face. His chest moved as if a set of powerful bellows was working under his shirt. "Put that shotgun down, or so help me . . ."

"You'll do what, Dawes? Near as I can tell, things didn't start going to shit until you ran them into the ground!"

"We had our chance tonight, but it's gone," Dawes said. His bulky frame remained steady as an oak. "I'm running this show and I'll bury you if I please. You may not be all there, but you gotta know that much is true."

Lem shifted from one foot to another. His face kept

twitching as if his spectacles were causing light from the nearby torches to scorch his eyes. Finally, he swung his shotgun away from Dawes and pointed it back to Slocum.

In a blur of motion, Slocum drew the Colt and aimed it at one of the glass circles over Lem's eye. "You men obviously got your own problems, but I don't take kindly to being at the end of a shotgun."

"Are you gonna help us or not?" Lem asked.

Slocum glanced between Mark and Dawes. It was tough to pick which of those two was in charge of the others, but it sure as hell wasn't Lem. "What did this Banner do to you men anyway?"

"What does it matter?" Mark asked.

"I'd say it matters quite a bit since you all seem so anxious to put Banner down. Or should I say . . . put her down?"

"Either way would be right," Dawes replied.

"Then that would be a problem," Slocum said. "I may be old-fashioned, and I'm not partial to killing women."

"What about lying, thieving bitches?" Lem asked. "You mind putting down one of those?"

Slocum took a moment to look at the three men in front of him. Although they were still carrying their guns out for everyone to see, he could tell they weren't going to pull their triggers right away. If that wasn't the case, they would have started firing long ago. Glancing at either side of the street, Slocum could also see a few more folks trying to see what was going on. None of them seemed prepared to interfere, but were all eager to see another dustup.

"If you won't tell me what the problem is," Slocum said, "then you must be willing to pay a good amount to get the job done."

"Depends on how well it all turns out."

Slocum grinned and shook his head. "You must be new to this, big man. Jobs like this require payment in advance."

Dawes let out a breath and looked around at the folks that were closing in on all sides. Apparently drawing the same conclusions as Slocum about the intentions of the crowd, the big fellow waved them all away as if he was erasing a chalk-board. "We got all the guns we need," he said to Slocum. "Sorry to bust into your room, but it was a mistake. If that ain't good enough for you, then that's tough shit."

Holstering the Colt, Slocum said, "Apology accepted."

Dawes grumbled something or other, but Slocum couldn't make much of it. When the big man turned his back to Slocum and walked away, Mark fell into step beside him. Lem wasn't quite so quick to move, however, He kept his shotgun at hip level as a passing breeze caused some of the long, greasy strings of his hair to drift into his face.

"Best not follow us again," Lem warned.

Chuckling under his breath, Slocum replied, "I already see following you the first time was a mistake."

"Yer damn right it was." With that, Lem trotted back a few steps before turning and rushing to catch up with the other two men. He was pleased enough with himself to dis-regard Slocum well before he was out of the Colt Navy's range. Fortunately for the bespectacled man, Slocum wasn't inclined to put a bullet into a man's back. Not yet anyway.

Ignoring the stares and occasional hoots from the locals gathered along the street, Slocum retraced his steps back to the Crippled Mule Saloon. Once it became clear that no lead was going to fly, the crowd found other things to do and let Slocum go without much fuss. The faded paint on the front window of the Crippled Mule was in Slocum's sight when he heard an unfamiliar voice barking at him.

"You there! Don't take another step!"

The street was fairly busy in front of the saloon, so Slocum took his chances by pretending he hadn't heard the gruff voice. Before he made it another two feet toward the Mule's front door, Slocum heard that same voice from the street. This time, however, it was coming from a lot closer than it had been the first time around.

"I said not another step, mister," the voice demanded. "And don't make a move toward that pistol or I'll drop you where you stand."

Slocum turned around with his eyes cast at a slightly downward angle. That way, he was able to see the front of the other man's shirt before he could see his face. Just as he'd expected, Slocum spotted the dented badge pinned to the gruff man's pocket.

"Something I can do for you?" Slocum asked.

Now that he had Slocum's attention, the lawman planted his feet and propped his hands upon his hips. "There sure is. You can tell me why the second floor of that saloon is all shot to hell."

"Did you manage to track me down or did you just decide to look official after finishing your drink?"

The lawman looked to be somewhere in his mid-forties and had a wide face that was covered with at least two days' worth of stubble. His torso was thick as an old tree trunk, but some of that had to do with eating too much town food instead of any kind of muscle built up by living out on the trail. "I beg your pardon?" the lawman snapped.

"Never mind. What's on your mind, Sheriff?"

"I see you can read the badge, so you must not be stupid. Perhaps you're just a wiseass."

Slocum couldn't dispute either claim, but he sure as hell wasn't about to apologize for his tone. He'd seen plenty of lawmen and only a few of them were worth more than the metal it took to forge their badges. From what he'd seen so far, this lawman wasn't on the road to changing that opinion.

"Where'd you rush off to?" the sheriff asked.

"Stretching my legs."

"After shooting up the second floor of that saloon?"

"Who told you that?" Slocum asked.

"Plenty of folks heard those shots and plenty more saw you stomp out of there before the smoke had cleared."

"Did any of them tell you I was the one doing the shooting? If they did, they're damn liars!"

The lawman didn't have a quick answer for that one. He nodded once and held up his hands before tempers got any more frayed than they already were. "Every account in there puts you on the receiving end of those shots instead of the one pulling the trigger," the sheriff admitted. "Since it looks like the only thing you were sure to put on correctly was your gun belt, my guess is that you took off after the men that did the shooting. Am I right?"

Nodding once, Slocum said, "More or less."

"Then maybe you could tell me who they are or where they went."

"I don't know who they are, apart from a few first names. Dawes, Lem, and Mark. As for where they went," Slocum added as he pointed a finger back in the direction from which he'd come, "it was thataway."

The sheriff turned to look in that direction, but only saw a few tired horses walking down the street and an amused drunk lying against a water trough. When he turned back around, he was just in time to watch Slocum step back into the saloon.

3

"Sheriff's lookin' for ya," the barkeep hollered as Slocum walked by.

Slocum kept on walking. "I know," he said as he started climbing the stairs.

"I don't want my place shot up anymore tonight!"

"Fine by me."

When Slocum got to the top of the stairs, he found a mess of splinters on the floor and the stench of burnt gunpowder to mark the spot where all the shooting had taken place. His door swung on a busted hinge and his room was a mess. "At least nobody took my things," Slocum grumbled after he'd spotted his saddlebags lying in the same spot where he'd left them.

Slocum heard a few soft footsteps behind him. If Alice didn't favor rosewater perfume so much, he might have reacted out of instinct before hearing the soft voice in his ear. "Of course nobody's gonna steal your things," Alice said. "After the way you tore out of here, folks were just as scared of you as they were of them other three."

Slocum reached up to grab the hand that had snaked its way around his chest from behind. Keeping hold of her, he turned around to face Alice. "I'll need another room," he said. "This one's busted."

Alice grabbed his shirt with one hand and wrapped her other arm around Slocum's elbow. "I've got just the place," she told him as she dragged him a bit farther down the hall. "My room's nice and quiet, but I doubt it'll stay that way for long."

Draping his saddlebags over his shoulder, Slocum took another glance about to see if he'd left anything else behind. "If it's all the same to you, it's been a hell of a night and I—"

"No need to tell me that," Alice cut in as she shoved Slocum into her room and pushed the door shut behind them. "I saw every second of it and I'll be thinking about it for a long time. All these other idiots ran like chickens when the shooting started, but you just got all riled up. I've never seen the like! Even when that shotgun went off, I was so scared, but not you."

Shaking his head, Slocum could feel the excitement wearing into his bones as his ears rang from all that gunfire. "Yeah, it was something. I'd really like to just . . . what are you doing?"

Looking down, Slocum found Alice pulling down his jeans and reaching inside them. She smiled and her eyes widened once her fingers wrapped around his thick member. "You know what I'm doing," she said as he grew harder within her grasp. "Feels like you may even approve."

"The sheriff was after me and he'll probably be pestering me again real soon."

Alice lifted her skirts and gathered them up around her waist. "Oh, I'm sure," she mused as she guided him between her legs. She wasn't wearing any undergarments, so Slocum immediately felt her wetness once she started grinding her hips against him.

When he'd entered the saloon, his intention was to get a drink and lock himself in a room where he could hear himself think for a few minutes.

When he'd gotten up the stairs, Slocum just wanted some peace and quiet.

Now . . .

"Aw, hell," he grumbled as he gave in and reached beneath Alice's skirts to grab her round ass and pull her closer.

Slocum woke up with one leg hanging over the side of Alice's bed and the taste of whiskey in the back of his throat. He'd gotten his liquor the night before, but it happened somewhere in the middle of rustling the sheets with Alice, so it hadn't exactly been the relaxing drink he'd been after. Then again, he wasn't about to complain.

Sitting up and then swinging his other leg over the edge of the lumpy mattress, Slocum rubbed the back of his head and pulled in a breath. The soft glow of dawn was leaking in through the window, combining with the whiskey fog in his head to make Slocum wonder if he needed a new set of eyes. A few more breaths went a little ways in clearing his head, but the scent of coffee went a hell of a lot further.

"Rise and shine," Alice announced as she stepped into the room carrying a steaming mug in each hand. "I brought you some coffee."

"I know," Slocum said as he reached for one of the mugs. "It smells damn good."

"If you want breakfast, you'll have to drag yourself downstairs for it. You may be getting special treatment, but I draw the line at serving breakfast in bed."

"Fair enough," Slocum chuckled. "I intended on stretching my legs a bit anyhow."

"I'd like to recommend breakfast here, but I couldn't do that with a clear conscience. This saloon barely gets the whiskey right. The food's enough to put a man six feet under."

Slocum pulled on his clothes and buckled his gun belt around his waist. By the time he set his hat on top of his head, Alice had already tossed him a quick wave, blown him a kiss, and gone out the door. He picked up his saddlebags from where he'd dropped them the night before, hefted them over his shoulder, and walked out of the room. Out of curiosity, he stopped at his original room and tapped his toe against the bottom of the door. It swung open without much effort, but the broken hinge screamed like a stuck pig.

Slocum walked into his room and poked around for a minute or two. The place was a mess, but no more of a mess than when he'd left it the night before. Since he hadn't left any of his belongings in there, Slocum walked out and headed down the stairs.

The saloon was only slightly less busy than it had been the previous night. There were even a few familiar drunks still crumpled in the same chairs they'd planted themselves in before. Upon reaching the bar, Slocum knocked a few times to catch the attention of the man tending it. The morning barkeep was an older fellow who looked as if he would have been more comfortable behind a bank teller's cage.

"Can I help you, sir?" the bartender asked.

Slocum returned the older man's friendly smile and said, "The name's John Slocum. I—"

"I know who you are, sir. You've been staying here for a while."

Squinting a bit, Slocum sifted through his head for any recollection of the barkeep's face. He came up short, but that wasn't much of a surprise. Every other morning, he'd come down from his room using a set of narrow steps that led straight down to the back alley. He hadn't needed Alice's warning to put him off the Crippled Mule's food. All he'd needed was a nose that told him it was preferable to smell a bit of trash and walk through a dirty alley so long as he was able to avoid the stench of burnt oatmeal and sour drunks that wafted up from the saloon in the morning hours.

"Sheriff Maykin's been looking for you, sir," the barkeep said, giving voice to the very reason why Slocum had decided to walk down the main stairs this morning instead of his normal route.

After looking around, Slocum asked, "Is he here?"

"No, sir. He comes by for his morning coffee and leaves, which is what he did this morning. If you want to catch up to him—"

"I don't."

Smirking at the flustered tone in Slocum's voice, the barkeep replied, "If you change your mind, his office is on the far side of Carter Street. It's close to the blacksmith and that row of seamstress shops. There's also a real good place that serves breakfast on the opposite end of that street."

"The quiet part of town, huh? Why doesn't that surprise me?"

"He did want to have a word with you, but I don't think it was anything you should be worried about. He didn't even want to go up and wake you when he stopped by."

Slocum realized the old bartender was talking to him like a grandparent soothing a vexed young boy. Oddly enough, the old man had enough sincerity in his tone to keep that from grating on Slocum's nerves. Rather than take offense to being all but patted on the head, Slocum nodded and asked, "Do I owe anything for my stay here? I'd like to settle up."

Even as the bartender checked a tattered ledger that was kept under a rack of bottles nailed to the wall, he was shaking his head. Once he found the page he was after, he tapped it and thumped the ledger shut. "Nope. Your room, meals, and whiskey were courtesy of the house. If the owner has any problem with that, he'll answer to me for it."

"Much obliged," Slocum said as he tipped his hat.

Just then, the bartender snapped his fingers and reached beneath the bar again. "A lady left a note for you. She said you'd know what it's about."

Slocum took the folded scrap of paper and tucked it into his pocket. He knew it was Alice letting him know either where to meet her later that night or what she was going to do to him when she got her hands on him again. Either way, Slocum figured it could wait until after he'd stowed his gear and gotten some food in his belly.

The moment Slocum walked through the doors of the restaurant the bartender had recommended, he wanted to kick himself for not going there every morning he'd been in town. Smells drifted through the air that made his mouth water and his stomach grumble. Then again, it probably didn't help things that he hadn't eaten properly for the better part of a day.

The only open table was directly in front of a window facing the street. Even though Slocum wasn't expecting any trouble, it just didn't sit right for him to put himself on display like that. Fortunately, he only had to wait another few minutes before another table opened up that allowed him to put his back to a wall. Within seconds after he'd settled into his chair, a pretty young lady with short brown hair and a bright smile came over to greet him.

"Good morning to you," she said cheerily. "Want some coffee before I try to scrounge up a menu?"

"I think I can save you the trouble," Slocum told her. "Do I smell ham cooking?"

She nodded once. "Yep. Ham steak and fried eggs. That's our special."

"Biscuits?"

"Fresh ones."

"I'll take the special, extra biscuits, and some of that coffee."

Smiling even wider, the waitress rubbed his shoulder and said, "You're the best customer I've had all day. Be right back."

Slocum leaned back in his chair and gazed out the window. From his view, the town of East Padre actually seemed like a nice place to be. There were a few shops opening up for business across the street, plenty of people walking back and forth along the boardwalk, and a few carriages slowly ambling by. As the smell of coffee became stronger, Slocum's spirits lifted even more.

"Perfect timing," he said. "I was just about to hunt you

down." When he turned toward the scent of coffee, Slocum didn't find the waitress standing there with his cup. Instead, he found a taller woman with longer, darker hair looking back at him.

The woman wore a dark blue dress with a skirt that came all the way down to her heels, yet somehow still managed to give Slocum plenty to look at. The material was simple cotton, but was cut so that it hugged her hips to show a shapely set of curves. The news only got better as Slocum let his eyes wander above her waist. The bodice of her dress wrapped around a tight midsection and white laces crossed over a pair of firm breasts. She kept smiling at him in a way that let Slocum know she was aware he'd been sizing her up and wasn't about to object to it. In fact, she shifted on her feet in a way that moved her hips nicely.

"Sorry," Slocum said. "I thought you were the waitress."

"Really? And here I thought this dress would set me apart from the hired help."

Slocum chuckled and stood up to pull back the empty chair at his table. When the tall woman sat down, Slocum could see the waitress standing behind her holding a coffee cup. This time, the brown-haired young lady was not smiling.

"Can I get something for you, miss?" the waitress asked.

The taller woman smirked as if she could feel the consternation on the waitress's face even though she wasn't looking at her. "Just some tea, if you have it."

"I can find some," the waitress grumbled. "That is what the hired help is for, isn't it?"

"Yes. I suppose it is."

No matter how many fights he'd seen that involved fists or guns, Slocum still found the barbed comments from an angry woman to carry a sting of their own. In a way, he'd rather be in a regular sort of fight. At least there was an easy way out of those.

After the waitress had left, Slocum said, "You might not want to drink whatever she boils in along with that tea."

"I wasn't planning on it." Reaching across the table, she added, "My name is Eliza."

"John," Slocum replied as he shook her hand. The lady's grip was strong, but not so much so that she was putting on a show of strength. Her strength was there without being displayed.

"John Slocum," Eliza said. "Am I right?"

"You sure are. Have we met?"

"Not until just now. Actually, I heard about your little run-in with Mark, Dawes, and that other one that nips at his heels."

"Big news for a place like this?" Slocum asked.

"Loud news anyway. Did you get my note?"

That one caught Slocum off his guard for a moment. His eyebrows went up and his hand reflexively went to his shirt pocket. He removed the folded piece of paper he'd been given and nodded slowly. "I got it, but I haven't had a chance to read it."

Eliza smiled and started to talk, but stopped herself when she saw the waitress approach the table carrying a cup and a teapot.

When Slocum heard the sound of shattering glass, his first guess was that the waitress had dropped the teapot. But the sound hadn't come from where the waitress was standing. Instead, it came from the window. More specifically, the sound was the window itself shattering, followed by a few more cups breaking as people knocked into their tables so they could get down.

Slocum was still sorting through the confusion in his head when his body reacted to the immediate threat. Pointing his head to a spot between Eliza and the waitress, he leapt over and then extended his arms away from his body to catch both women. One arm hit Eliza across her upper chest, while Slocum's other arm knocked into the waitress's stomach. It wasn't very elegant, but the move served well enough to bring both women to the floor as more glass was shattered and bullets were shot through the air.

The hissing sound of flying lead was all too familiar to Slocum's ears. It was loud enough that he knew those bullets would have done some real damage if he hadn't cleared a path for them. Even though the women were squirming beneath his arms, Slocum pressed them down flat against the floor until the barrage let up for a second or two.

"Stay down," Slocum said to both women. Since it seemed to be good advice for more than the two ladies, he raised his voice and shouted so everyone in the place could hear him. "Everyone keep your heads down!"

Some of the folks did as they were told, but they were too petrified to have moved anyway. The rest of the diners were so spooked that they bolted for the front door. Some of them even headed for the kitchen in their haste to get the hell away from the front window.

Slocum wasn't any of those folks' keeper, so he kept his mind on the task at hand, got to his feet, and pulled the Colt Navy from its cross-draw holster. The pistol cleared leather and fit in Slocum's grip like an extension of his own hand. He kept his head down as he made his way to the side wall and followed it toward the shattered front window. Once he got a clear look at the street, he saw Lem standing there with his shotgun held in an easy, two-handed grip.

This time, Slocum didn't wait to see if Lem would fire. He pulled himself away from the window and gritted his teeth in expectation. Sure enough, the shotgun roared and blasted a sizable chunk from the window's frame. Slocum stepped from behind his cover and moved outside with his pistol ready. Dawes stood in the street a little ways behind Lem. Although he couldn't spot Mark right away, Slocum figured the third man was nearby. Both of the gunmen spotted Slocum and shifted their aim toward him.

Swearing under his breath, Slocum fired a few shots as he ducked back so there were some solid wood planks between him and the street. Even as he fired toward the gunmen, he knew those shots weren't going to hit their targets. They were too quick and too wild for anything but blind luck to guide them home. Slocum held his position for a second or two before hopping back into the line of fire to catch the men outside by surprise.

Apparently, Slocum's gamble had been a good one. The startled expressions on the gunmen's faces showed that they hadn't expected Slocum to show himself so soon. Even so, they quickly adjusted their aim while backing toward the other side of the street.

"You want a fight?" Slocum shouted. "Come and get it!" He fired until the hammer of his Colt Navy slapped against the back of an empty bullet casing. The smoke was thick in the air, but he was able to herd the gunmen away from the crowded restaurant. He also knew he'd hit pay dirt on at least one of his shots since Dawes was cussing up a storm and hobbling into the open doorway of a shop across from the restaurant.

Glancing about, Slocum caught sight of Mark and Lem poking their heads from behind the cover they'd managed to get to. Allowing his reflexes to take over, Slocum dropped straight down and rolled toward the street. Another shotgun blast roared through the air and a few stray pellets of buckshot ripped into the ground where Slocum had previously been standing. Gritting his teeth while continuing to move, Slocum pulled fresh bullets from his gun belt and reloaded the Colt.

Another barrage of shots was fired, but it didn't come from Dawes, Lem, or Mark. Instead, it came from farther down the street and was being fired by a small group of men who were heading toward the restaurant. Slocum spotted them just as he'd finished reloading.

"Throw down your guns or we'll kill all three of you!" the sheriff hollered as he and some of his men fanned out to move toward Dawes and the rest like a wall of bad intentions.

Slocum remained on his belly to keep from giving any of the gunmen a clean shot at him. Of course, he didn't have the best firing angle from that spot either.

Dawes, Mark, and Lem pulled their triggers as fast as

they could to start a hailstorm of lead that filled the entire
street. Slocum fired back a few times, which was just enough
to force the others away from him. The gunfire only lasted a
few seconds. During that time, Dawes and the other two fled
down the street and rounded a corner.

4

After the thunder had faded, Slocum spotted something on the ground in front of him. It was the letter that he'd been carrying in his pocket. Now it lay on the street, getting ready to be carried away by a passing breeze. Slocum snatched up the letter. The paper had straightened out a bit, allowing him to get a look at the flowing handwriting covering most of that side. His eyes drifted to the biggest lettering on the page, which was the signature at the bottom.

The name was Eliza Banner.

"Of course," Slocum grumbled.

"I said drop the gun!" the sheriff barked as he moved in closer to the restaurant.

Calmly folding up the paper using one hand, Slocum dropped his gun into its holster. "Late again, Sheriff," he said.

"We'll see about that. You two," the lawman said as he glanced at a pair of his deputies, "go fetch those other three and bring them back to my office."

The two younger lawmen rushed down the street, leaving one more deputy to stand beside the sheriff.

"I'll need that gun, mister," the sheriff said.

Before Slocum could comply, or even let the lawman know what he thought about his request, folks began trickling out from the restaurant. Some of them were anxious to get the hell away from there, while a few of them had their own guns drawn. The ones that were heeled made their way over to stand at Slocum's side.

"Did you get any of them?" one of the armed folks asked.

Another fellow from the restaurant, an older man carrying a rusty .44, spat on the ground before tucking his pistol under his belt. "Damn fine job!" he said to Slocum. Shifting his eyes to the lawmen, he added, "Did you see that, Sheriff? Hell of a show! Sheriff Maykin?"

"Yeah, I saw it," the sheriff snapped. "I was just about to resolve the situation."

The old-timer with the .44 looked back and forth between Slocum and the lawmen. Finally, he shrugged and said, "Seems to be resolved to me."

"Me, too," Slocum said.

The sheriff desperately wanted to relieve Slocum of his gun and possibly even haul him down to the jail for proper questioning. Slocum could tell that much just by looking at the frustration boiling behind the sheriff's eyes. Maykin's lips pressed together into a tight line and his brow furrowed intently. The more folks from the restaurant gathered to give their thanks to Slocum, the closer the sheriff got to shooting steam from his ears.

Finally, one of the locals walked past the sheriff, patted him on the shoulder, and said, "You should deputize that man."

Sheriff Maykin didn't say anything to that. All he did was nod and wait for the people to clear out. After a few more seconds had passed, his deputy leaned over and asked, "Do you still want to arrest him, Sheriff?"

"No, I don't want to arrest him," Maykin replied. "All I wanted was to ask him some questions."

"You don't think your deputies could use any help?" Slocum asked.

Suddenly, the sheriff's eyes widened and he looked down at the other end of the street. "Just don't go anywhere," he said to Slocum. "Now that everything's under control here, I'll go lend my boys a hand."

Slocum stepped back to let the two lawmen hurry past him. He did his best not to chuckle, but someone else wasn't holding themselves back so well.

"Seeing that man do his job makes me think about taking a run at this town's bank," Eliza said as she stepped over to Slocum. "With that kind of law around here, a gang of children should be able to rob the place without firing a shot."

"With that kind of law around here," Slocum replied, "anyone with any money at all would know well enough to look after it themselves."

"Good point. You did a fine job by the way."

Slocum turned around to face her. Eliza stood almost as tall as he did, but part of that could have been due to the heels of her boots. Even so, she was a statuesque woman who looked even better when the wind came along to rustle a few strands of her long, black hair. She kept her arms crossed and one hip cocked to the side as if she was relaxing in the corner of a warm room instead of standing in a dirty street with the scent of burnt powder still hanging in the air.

"If I'd finished the job last night, none of those assholes would be around to keep firing shots at me," Slocum said.

"You might still be able to catch them," she offered.

"They may not be the sharpest tools in the shed, but I'd wager they've already got a plan on getting out of here after firing those shots. I don't know this town well enough to come up with a way to circle around or guess where they'd be headed. Since they've got to be looking for men coming straight after them, following them directly would be a real good way to run directly into another round of gunshots."

As if on cue, a shotgun blast as well as several pistol shots sounded in the distance from the direction Dawes and his men had gone.

"See?" Slocum asked. "Looks like those lawmen just proved my point."

Eliza nodded approvingly as she looked down the street.

When she locked eyes with Slocum again, she was smiling a bit. "Seems like this isn't the first time you've been shot at."

"Nope, and I doubt it'll be the last."

"You think those law dogs will round them up?"

"Not my problem," Slocum replied. With that, he tipped his hat, put his back to the commotion, and started walking down the street. He smirked to himself when Eliza fell into step beside him.

"Mind if I come along with you?" she asked.

"Not a bit."

"Did you read my note?"

"I've been a little busy."

Eliza shot a quick glance over her shoulder at the shattered front window of the restaurant. Folks were still gathered in front of the place, but most of them were finding other places to go to. That left the restaurant's owner to stand in front of his place and loudly lament the damage to his window. Looking back at Slocum, Eliza asked, "Do you always leave your mark like that?"

"This wasn't exactly my doing, but yeah. Things do seem to get lively when I stay put for too long. That's why I intend on moving along."

"Getting away from East Padre before those gunmen get a clean shot?"

"If I was too worried about those idiots, I would have chased them down myself."

"You mean you won't be chasing them down?" Eliza asked with a sly grin.

Eventually, Slocum replied, "I'll catch up to them soon enough."

"I'd like to be there to see that."

"I bet you would, Miss Banner. They were interested enough to follow you around until you settled in for breakfast."

The two of them had walked down the street and made it to the corner. It wasn't far from where they'd started, but folks seemed to have already forgotten where they'd come from or what had just happened a few minutes ago. Slocum had seen plenty of places like that, where gunfire was treated with the same amount of interest as the occasional rumble of thunder. Both would attract a few half-interested glances, but neither was anything new. If there was no rain or dead bodies in the street, folks just went about their business. There would be another storm soon enough.

"So those men were after me?" Eliza asked innocently.

Slocum shook his head and laughed under his breath. "If you mean to jerk me around, you can just keep on walking, Miss Banner."

"Call me Eliza."

"All right," Slocum said as he turned to face her head-on. "You can just keep on walking, *Eliza*. Now, if you'll excuse me, I've got some supplies to purchase."

As Slocum crossed the street and rounded the corner, Eliza kept pace with him. Her long legs closed the distance between them with little effort. Her skirts rustled about her ankles as she pulled them up enough to keep her sleek black boots from snagging on the fluttering material.

"Those men were after me, Mr. Slocum," she said.

"I know."

"You chased them down once already. How close did you get?"

Without breaking stride, Slocum replied, "Close enough to have a chat with them. Close enough for them all to take a shot at me if that's what they'd wanted to do."

"They didn't mind shooting at you today."

"I doubt they even knew I was in that restaurant."

"They could have killed plenty of other people with all that shooting. For all I know, they hit a cartload of innocents when they—"

"If you want to report your concerns, go find the sheriff," Slocum interrupted. "Otherwise, you can stop trying to convince me that someone needs to put those assholes in their place."

"Great. Now can I convince you to ride along with me as I head into the Arizona Territory?"

Slocum nodded and started ambling toward the row of general stores at a more leisurely pace. "There it is. Finally! I was wondering if you'd make your point before or after I was in the middle of paying for my bacon and jerky."

"If you would have read my note, you wouldn't have had to wait so long."

"Funny. You don't strike me as the sort of woman who would be so slow to speak her mind."

"I speak my mind plenty," Eliza told him. "Some subjects are just a little more sensitive than others."

Raising his eyebrows a bit, Slocum said, "Now you went and piqued my interest. Why don't you tell me what you want to tell me while I get my provisions?"

"I'd rather not talk where just anyone can hear."

"If the folks around here lost interest in a shooting so quickly, I doubt you'll draw much attention just by talking."

"It's not the locals that concern me," Eliza said. "There are a few people other than those three gunmen that I'm worried about. The problem is, I don't know exactly who else could have been hired to act as my shadow."

"And if one of these wrong people hear what you want to say, that would be bad?" Slocum asked in a somewhat teasing manner.

Eliza grinned playfully and narrowed her eyes in a way that made her look like a coy predator. It was an odd combination that didn't seem to mesh, but she somehow pulled it off anyway. "Yes, Mr. Slocum. It would be bad."

Fishing the paper from his pocket, he held it between two fingers and asked, "Everything's in this note?"

"Not quite everything, but enough to give you an idea if you'd rather talk to me again or not."

Just looking at the seductive curl of her lips and the trim lines of her body was enough for Slocum to know he wanted to talk to her again. Going into business for more than the things that immediately came to mind, however, was something else. If she'd approached him in a different manner, he might very well have sent her on her way no matter how well she looked when she did it. Slocum was intrigued by her and, judging by the mischievous grin on her face, Eliza knew it.

Flipping the paper between his fingers a few times, Slocum kept it folded and said, "Give me a hint."

"You know those men are after me, Mr. Slocum. You know they're dangerous. Do you really need a hint as to what I might want from you?"

Slocum stepped onto the boardwalk, which was raised less than a foot off the uneven ground. Since the shopkeepers seemed to care more about their places than the saloon owners, the boardwalk wasn't as cracked and warped as it was in front of the Crippled Mule. After setting both feet onto the fresh lumber, Slocum said, "Indulge me."

Eliza let out a flustered breath and glanced back and forth. There were a few people stepping from the store who were reluctant to cut off the conversation they were having with someone inside the shop. Leaning forward and dropping her voice to a harsh whisper, she said, "I'm traveling to the Arizona Territory and I don't want to do it alone."

"Try the railroad," Slocum replied in a whisper that matched Eliza's.

"Too easy for someone to follow me."

"Then what about a stagecoach?"

She shook her head again. "Same thing. Also, someone could just stop the coach anywhere along the line and . . . well . . . do whatever they wanted."

Slocum leaned in a little closer. Thanks to a breeze that brushed Eliza's hair toward him, he was able to feel the soft strands touch his cheek and to catch the sweet scent of her skin. "I think those three men have bigger problems than you right now." Once that was said, Slocum backed away and stepped into the store.

It was a little shop that was broken into several neat rows

of tables. At the back of the place were sacks of grain, flour, and sugar, all piled into symmetrical stacks. At the front of the shop, right next to the door, was a short counter. A plump woman sat perched upon a tall stool behind the counter. Behind her was a cash register that looked heavier than an anvil.

Slocum tipped his hat to the clerk and got a warm, beaming smile in return. Her hair was graying around the edges and was pulled back into a braid. The bright yellow bonnet on the clerk's head made her look even sunnier.

"Lovely morning!" she chirped.

"A bit loud, but yes," Slocum replied.

The clerk's smile didn't even begin to fade as she quickly waggled her hand toward the door. "Those saloons are always rowdy, but it's usually just a bunch of noise. You're perfectly safe in the shopping district."

"The law makes sure of that?"

Shrugging slightly, the woman let her eyes drift down to the counter in front of her. Slocum followed her line of sight all the way down to a shotgun that was propped behind the counter where the woman could easily reach it.

"The sheriff makes his rounds," she said. "But we do just fine on our own."

"That's the best way to go about things," Slocum said.

Even though it hadn't seemed possible, the woman's smile beamed even brighter. "That's precisely what my Earl always says!"

"Earl sounds like a wise man."

"Most definitely. Can I help you find anything or are you just looking around?"

"I need some food and supplies, seeing as how I'll be leaving soon."

"Right along that wall," the clerk told him. "Since you're such a nice man, I'll even throw in a few of my sugar cookies. Baked fresh this morning."

"Much obliged, ma'am."

Within seconds after Slocum had walked toward the spot

where the clerk had pointed, he heard the bell over the shop's front door jingle. The cheerful clerk tried to make some small talk, but whoever had come inside wasn't having any of it. Before too long, Slocum heard the tap of polished boots approaching him.

"I'm not just worried about those three," Eliza said, picking up exactly where the conversation had left off.

"You could always write me another letter," Slocum offered.

Eliza hurried around him to stand in front of Slocum. Once there, she planted her feet and put her hands upon her hips defiantly. "I have tried to be polite, Mr. Slocum, but you seem to enjoy spinning me in circles."

"Do I?"

"Yes. I believe you do."

After a few seconds of thinking it over, Slocum shrugged. "Yeah, I suppose I do. After all the gunfire that's been coming my way, it's proven to be a nice distraction."

"Why won't you hear me out?"

"Because I don't like wasting my time on folks that don't just spit out what they want to say," Slocum told her as he made his way from one table to another while gathering the supplies he was after. "Those gunmen shoot at me for no good reason, the sheriff treats me like a criminal, and you expect me to read up on you before you'll have a real conversation. I don't have time for any of it, so I think I'll just move along."

"What about those men that shot at you?" Eliza asked. "Are you just going to let that pass?"

The smile that the clerk had put onto Slocum's face dimmed a bit. "That's my business," he said.

"It's my business too, Mr. Slocum. And if we work together, we can both stand to make a good amount of money. If the wrong set of ears gets wind of what we're doing, however, our business could get real messy real quick."

Slocum had his arms loaded with coffee, sugar, cans of peaches and beans, as well as some soap for his saddle. "Well, why didn't you just put it that way before?" he asked. "That would have cut down on a lot of aggravation."

Eliza started to respond to that, but wound up letting out a long, flustered breath.

Slocum continued down the row of tables. "And one more thing," he said. "Call me John."

5

Aunty Mae's was on the opposite end of town from the saloons of Second Street. Even though the sign over the door advertised billiards, there was only one billiard table, which seemed to have been abandoned long ago. The felt was dusty and the balls looked as if they hadn't seen the outside of their rack for years, but Aunty Mae's was still fairly busy. All of the customers simply preferred to sit at the card tables that were scattered throughout the establishment.

It was well into the afternoon when Slocum finally walked into the place. In the time since he'd paid for his supplies, he'd kicked around the idea of renting another room for the night, but settled on sharing a stall with his horse. He'd already dropped his saddlebags into a corner of that stall, so he piled his supplies there as well. For some reason, the horse he'd ridden into East Padre was fidgety around most anyone but Slocum. The stable man had picked up on it right away and refused to so much as brush the animal for an additional fee. For that reason, Slocum had felt just fine in scattering a bunch of loose hay over the supplies and leaving them in the rear corner of the stall. The horse was as good a guard as any.

Although his intentions had been to wrap up his business

and leave town before the sun went down, Slocum had to admit that he was enjoying Aunty Mae's. It definitely wasn't the biggest place in town, but it was by far the calmest. Men drank their drinks while a piano was played somewhere in the back. Hostesses drifted between the tables to offer their company, and not one fight had broken out since Slocum had walked through the door. What else could he ask for?

"Care for a drink?" a buxom hostess wrapped up in black lace and dark red velvet asked.

"Whiskey," Slocum said.

"You new here?"

"Yep."

"Then the first one's on the house. Aunty Mae's tradition."

Chalk another one up for Aunty Mae.

Picking out a table with a good view of both entrances to the place, Slocum leaned back in a chair and kicked his feet up onto another one. The free whiskey was so good that Slocum wound up buying an entire bottle. It wasn't cheap, but after downing a few shots of the stuff, he wasn't in the mood to complain. As he tipped the bottle to refill his glass, he saw a familiar face enter the room and quickly pick out his table.

Eliza had changed into a different dress that was darker in color and had a slit that ran up along the side of the skirt to display the sleek, muscular tone of her legs. She still wore the high black boots, and she moved in them as if she'd been born with them laced around her narrow feet.

"Been waiting long, John?" she asked as she pulled up a chair so she didn't have to sit where his boots were resting.

"Just long enough to get a feel for this place."

"And?"

"And it sure beats the places I've been lately."

She smiled and folded her hands upon the table. "Good. Maybe we can stay for a while."

Slocum shook his head. "I'll keep this place in mind if I ever pass through this town again, but I won't be staying for long. You wanted to have a word with me somewhere away from prying ears, so have your words."

After glancing around to find everyone else was either involved in their own conversations or focused on their cards, Eliza let out a breath and placed both hands flat upon the table. "I haven't been in town for long. Before coming here, I was in Dallas."

"So you said in your letter."

"Oh," she said with genuine surprise. "You read it?"

"I had some time while I was waiting."

"So you know that I'm a gambler by trade."

Slocum angled his head slightly and shrugged his shoulders. "I don't know if I'd call that a trade as such, but go on."

The little sigh Eliza let out was enough to show her disagreement with Slocum's assessment, but she went on without disputing it any further. "I spent a lot of time in Texas. There was plenty of money to be made, plenty of games to play, and plenty of places to play them. More than enough to go around."

Slocum grinned and said, "There's never enough to satisfy everybody."

"Smart man," she said. "I started seeing one man at more and more of my games."

"Did you play or deal?" Slocum asked.

"I dealt faro when money was short, but I haven't had to do that for a while. I've been on a particularly good run in poker. A group came around to play in a high-stakes game that took place twice a week. My winnings weren't much by the other players' standards, but it was enough to keep me going."

Swinging his legs off the other chair, Slocum took a pull of his whiskey and said, "So let me guess. One of these rich fellas took offense to losing his money on a regular basis."

"His name's Armand Theil. He started threatening me and even tried to force himself on me. I got away, but I had to leave Dallas behind for good."

"Aren't gamblers always on the move for one reason or another?"

Eliza narrowed her eyes and dropped her voice to something just above a whisper. "You didn't strike me as the sort of man who approves of hurting women, John."

"I don't. I was talking about you as a gambler. Wouldn't you have left Dallas on your own before too long?"

"When he attacked me, it was the way some men insist on attacking women. That had nothing to do with me as a gambler."

Slocum didn't need to be a poker player to know that Eliza wasn't bluffing. Her voice was too serious to be anything but sincere, and the spark in her eyes told him that she was most definitely thinking about something specific that was like a fresh wound inside her.

"So he raped you? You don't strike me as the sort of woman who would stand for that."

Blinking as if that question had shaken her out of her previous state of mind, Eliza slowly shook her head. "He tried. I was able to kick him in the balls, get to my gun, and fend off his men."

"Sounds like you can take care of yourself," Slocum said.

"I suppose my lucky streak held that night, but after that he kept coming after me," Eliza explained. "Theil showed up at all my games and gave me a hard time. He was tight enough with the law in Dallas that he got away with trying to rape me. I even got a warning for kicking him and threatening to shoot his boys. Can you believe that?"

"Yeah," Slocum grumbled. "I can."

Eliza reached out to take a quick drink from Slocum's whiskey. She took the bottle, paused for a nod from him, and then took a drink. Setting it down, she continued talking as if the liquor was just a sip of water. "Theil always has gunmen with him. He said they were there to protect his money, but those men were killers plain and simple. I could see it in their eyes. He made it clear that he would get to me sooner or later. When he said it, he passed it off like he intended on winning back his money, but he and I both knew better than that. He wanted to get to *me,* not the money."

Slocum took a drink of whiskey and let out a slow breath

as the heat from the liquor made its way right down into the bottom of his gut. As the firewater burned through him, it also allowed him to sink a bit deeper into his chair as if a warm hand had loosened the knots in his muscles. "So this all just started happening all of a sudden?" he asked.

Eliza nodded. "I could tell he was sweet on me at first, but I didn't think it was anything too serious. Just flirting at the table between games. When he tried to force himself on me, he wasn't too happy to be turned away, and after that it got ugly."

"Armand Theil, huh?"

"Yes," she replied. "Have you ever heard of him?"

Slocum took a moment to let that name roll through his head. It didn't strike a chord, but that wasn't saying a whole lot. Plenty of men took a new name every time they got to a new town. Gamblers and gunfighters were especially known for that. Some of them relied upon their names and reputations to work to their advantage. Others did their best to keep folks from knowing who they were so they could avoid whatever trouble came along with who they were.

"None of the men that shot up my room called themselves by that name," he said. "And this is the first time I've heard it."

"I don't know if Theil is in town," Eliza said. "Those three that shot up the Crippled Mule and that restaurant this morning are on his payroll, though."

"So you were staying at the Crippled Mule as well?"

"Yes," she told him. "I was on my way back when they took a few shots at me on Second Street. I got away from them, circled around the place, and ducked into a whorehouse. Dawes must have thought I went back up to my room when he started kicking in doors. I suppose my lucky streak is still holding."

Slocum didn't put a lot of stock in luck. From his experience, luck was just another word for the natural flow of things. A man who kept his head straight and his powder dry could get through just about anything. He didn't need to rely upon blind chance to go his way. Sometimes, things happened to fall just the right way for a real good outcome to come about. Most of the times, it was safer to prepare for the worst. That wasn't good luck or bad luck. It was just the way things were.

"So your letter mentioned something about a business arrangement," Slocum said. "I think I know where you're headed, but why don't you tell me what you had in mind?"

Eliza pulled in a breath and glanced down at the bottle as if she was about to ask for another drink to steel her nerves. When she let out her breath, she found enough strength to continue without the dose of firewater to keep her going. "There's a big game being held in Bray. It's a—"

"It's a silver town in the Arizona Territory," Slocum cut in. "There used to be silver there anyway. Now it's overrun with saloons, whores, and cardplayers. Kind of like this place, but without the charm."

"It's not as bad as some of the towns on the gambling circuit, but it sure is a lot better since those twitchy miners packed up and moved on. They were good for some easy money, though. When was the last time you were there?"

Slocum blinked and moved his glass around to get some more whiskey sloshing about. "It was a while ago. I was one of the twitchy miners."

"You were a miner? I . . . wouldn't have guessed that."

"I've done plenty of jobs. At the time, that was what paid the most in that neck of the woods."

After pondering that for all of two seconds, Eliza shrugged and said, "I need to get to Bray, but I know Theil will also be there. Since he knows I'm coming, he'll surely have some hired guns to back his play. Probably more than the ones you've already seen."

"All that on your account?"

"Theil is a coward who won't face a woman unless he's sure she'll tremble and cry whenever he raises his voice. I'm not that sort, John. He knows I arm myself, so he's not going to take chances the next time he makes his play."

"What's so important about this game in Bray?" Slocum

asked. "If it's so dangerous, why not just sit out? I'm sure there's got to be other games all over the place. The Arizona Territory alone caters to plenty of gambling types."

This time, Eliza didn't just stare at the bottle of whiskey. She reached out and took hold of it before glancing at Slocum for permission. When she saw him nod at her silent request, she put her lips around the bottle and tipped it back to let a healthy dose of the whiskey rush down her throat. As with the first drink she'd taken, Eliza didn't even flinch before swallowing her share. She put the bottle down and then dabbed at her mouth. Looking up to meet Slocum's eyes, she said, "You're a gunfighter."

"If you say so."

She nodded confidently. "You're a fighting man and you know how to use that gun of yours. I could tell that much from what I've already seen."

"All right then."

"Even if you don't make your living by your gun, you must know how important your reputation is. A good reputation can go a long way. It speaks up for you when you're in trouble and it convinces folks to help you out when you need it."

"A man's reputation can also get him into trouble," Slocum said. "As for the rest of what you said, I suppose there's a bit of truth to it. What's your point?"

"When Theil couldn't have me for himself, he decided to ruin me. He swore as much, and has been following through whenever he could. When I didn't run away like a frightened little girl, he started talking tough during all those games he followed me to. When I still didn't back down, he made threats to kill me for stealing from him. When that didn't frighten me away, he hired his gunmen to do the job that he was still too yellow to do on his own."

Slocum listened to her carefully. More important than the words she was saying, he paid close attention to how she said those words. While plenty of what she told him made sense, there was still something missing. "You weren't frightened?" he asked.

"I didn't say that," she replied calmly. "I said I wasn't frightened away. I was frightened as anyone when they know their life is in danger. I just didn't give Theil the satisfaction of seeing me scamper off the way he wanted me to."

"So he pushed it further."

Eliza nodded again. "Maybe if I would have let him save face in front of his poker friends, things wouldn't have gotten so bad. He needed to look like a big man, so he kept pushing. He didn't expect me to hold my ground and when I did, he could either back off or push harder. He wasn't about to do the first, so he did the second."

"And I suppose you just . . . stayed strong and kept holding your ground."

Eliza flinched a bit when she heard the tone of Slocum's voice. She looked at him, and realized he was staring back at her with an equal amount of intensity. "I hired a few men of my own," she finally admitted. "But it looks like you already knew that."

"Not as such," Slocum said. "But I could tell things had gone a bit further than you were saying. There's blood between you and Theil. I may have just met you and never met him, but I can tell that much already. It's in the way you mention his name and it's in the way those other three were tearing through this town to get to you. Things got bad, didn't they?"

"Yes."

"How many?"

"Excuse me?" Eliza asked.

"How many died?" When he didn't get his answer right away, Slocum leaned forward and slapped his hand against the table. "You can bat your eyelashes at me all you want, but that don't mean I'm about to swallow whatever bullshit you try to feed me. All the double-talking tricks you know might go a long way with bad cardplayers. That pretty face may even get you out of a good amount of jams, but I've gotten in the middle of enough blood feuds to know when one's further along than what you're telling me. If you want anything from me, I won't go into it without knowing the lay of the land. If you don't want to tell me, you can aim those pretty eyes somewhere else."

Eliza paused to catch her breath. Although she did seem a bit taken aback by what Slocum had said, she didn't seem rattled. On the contrary, her cheeks flushed a bit and the corner of her mouth curled slightly into the faintest hint of a smile. "Four. That's how many have died so far, John. Four men that I know of."

"Men you hired?"

"The three I hired and one of his. It happened the first time Theil tried to take a run at me after a four-day-long poker game. Him and his boys walked straight at me when I was walking to my hotel, and then the men I hired closed in. There was a fight, but the men I hired turned out to be more bark than bite. They shot up plenty of men, including Theil himself, but only managed to kill one before they were all gunned down. That one was Theil's nephew. Ever since then, things have gotten a whole lot worse."

Slocum nodded slowly as he eased back into his seat. "Losing your own blood will do that."

"His nephew was a killer that was known all throughout West Texas."

"What was his name?"

"Jed Harbury."

Now that name did strike a chord with Slocum. He hadn't crossed paths with Jed Harbury, but he'd been asked to join up with a posse that was hunting him down. Considering how highly he regarded most lawmen, and considering that Harbury hadn't done a thing to him, Slocum had laughed in the face of the man who'd asked him to join that posse. Not too long ago, stories of Jed's exploits had stopped. Now Slocum knew why.

"So you lost your hired guns and Theil lost his nephew. Isn't that enough?" Slocum asked.

"This is a big game and a lot of big players will be going to Bray to play it," Eliza explained. "Theil will be spreading lies about me whether he wins or loses. Even if his bullshit only sticks to a few of those gamblers, it'll spread far and wide until I won't be able to get into a game worth more than three dollars."

"Rumors and reputation, huh?"

She nodded. "That's right." Eliza's expression brightened as she smirked and propped her elbows on the table. Setting her chin on the back of her folded hands, she added, "You could play in the game, too, you know. We could be a good team."

Leaning forward and lowering his voice to match Eliza's, Slocum said, "If I do this job, I'll get paid for it. Real money, not promises."

"You will, John. It's a big game."

"And every game's got its losers. You can't guarantee me that you won't be one of them."

"No, but I'm a hell of a player. I can turn a little money into a lot well enough. Considering how much money will be floating around Bray, it would only take a few good strikes to make a killing. You'll receive your piece as soon as it starts coming in."

That made Slocum laugh. As the laughter grew, he tipped his hat back and poured some more whiskey from his bottle. "You've got brass, lady, I'll give you that much. All this talk and all this propositioning and you don't even have enough to pay me for my trouble?"

"I've already tried hiring gunmen," she said without missing a beat. "They worked just hard enough to earn their fee."

"And then they got killed," Slocum pointed out.

"That's right. They got killed. I've also seen enough to know you're not going to be so reckless. If you were, you would have already tried to separate me from my money instead of genuinely trying to figure me out."

"I had you figured out while you were chasing me through that store and hounding me to read your letter. What I didn't have figured, I've cleared up by now."

Flattening her arms upon the table, Eliza sat bolt upright

in a true picture of propriety. "Is that so? And what have you figured out, John Slocum?"

"You're not quite a straight dealer, but you're close enough for my purposes. You're honest about getting to this game and you'll go there whether I decide to come along or not. You're also petrified of Armand Theil." Knowing his last few words had ruffled Eliza's feathers, Slocum held out a finger to freeze her before she could say anything in her defense. "Petrified," he repeated, "and there's nothing wrong with that. I believe your story about the blood that's been spilled and I'm actually considering your offer."

For a moment, Eliza looked as if she was ready to defend herself. When she realized she didn't have anything to defend against, she snapped her head back and asked, "Really? You're considering my offer? I won't be able to pay you much up front."

"I figured as much. Otherwise, you would have dangled the sum in front of me already. If I'm going to put myself on the line to protect you, I want two things. First of all, I'm to be your partner. Not just a hired gun."

"Done," she said with a curt nod.

"And second, I want some security that I'll get a real return."

Eliza grinned mischievously and looked over her shoulder at the other card tables. "I might just be able to arrange a demonstration for you."

6

Eliza sidled up to the card table like a cat slinking up to an unsuspecting mouse. Slocum had rarely seen a woman use so many muscles just walking from one spot to another. Every move she made was damn close to poetry. Her hips shifted back and forth. Her arms swayed just enough to get her shoulders rocking, which in turn got her breasts swaying just enough to catch any man's eye. As she circled around the table, Slocum was given a view of her backside and wasn't disappointed in the least.

"Hello there," she said in a way that was both friendly and seductive. "Mind if I sit in for a few hands?"

The three men at the table varied in age from early twenties to late fifties. The youngest fellow was first to jump up from his seat and motion toward one of the empty chairs. "Not at all, miss. Take a load off."

The man in between the other two looked to be in his late thirties, which made him just old enough to be wary while the younger man was eager. Eliza seemed to have picked up on this right away, and let her eyes linger upon that man for a few seconds longer than they had on the kid who'd invited her to sit.

"Hello there," she said to the wary man already seated at the table. "My name's Eliza. Who might you be?"

The suspicion in the man's eyes dimmed a bit. The tension in his face and shoulders vanished like smoke being waved away from a cooking fire. To Eliza's credit, she'd managed to do all of that with a subtle tone in her voice and a look in her eyes that would get any man hot under the collar.

"The name's Carter," the previously wary man said. "You're welcome to play, but the stakes have been getting a bit high."

Settling into her spot, Eliza nodded. "That shouldn't be too much of a problem. Is it all right if my friend joins us?"

The other three men glanced toward Slocum as if they hadn't even realized he was there. This was the spot where the younger man raised his hackles and the other two sized Slocum up quietly.

"Don't worry," Eliza said to the younger man. "He's not that close of a friend."

"Yeah?" the kid replied.

"Most definitely, Mister . . ."

"Oh . . . uhh . . ."

Since the kid was clearly flustered by Eliza's attention, the oldest gambler stepped in and said, "He's Joey and I'm Matt. You're Eliza, so that just leaves this man out in the cold."

"I'm John," Slocum announced. Since the others at the table were just fine using one name, he decided to follow suit. It was Eliza's show, after all, and he didn't want to influence anything by taking the chance that someone might recognize his name.

"Pleased to meet you, John," Matt said. "You always gamble while you're heeled?"

"I could ask the same question of him," Slocum replied as he glanced over at Carter.

Carter shrugged and shuffled the cards. "Long as he doesn't get drunk or rowdy, I don't have a problem."

"Me neither," Joey added, being sure to keep his eyes on Eliza. "I been in a whole lot rougher places than this and ain't never had a problem."

Although the other men at the table didn't seem impressed,

Eliza widened her eyes a bit and smiled as if she was looking at a decorated war hero. "How exciting," she said.

"Yeah," Carter grumbled. "Real exciting. Can we play now?"

There were nods all around, so Carter called out for the ante. It was five dollars. Since Slocum had spent most of his last few days eating cheap food and drinking free whiskey over at the Crippled Mule, he wasn't carrying much in the way of money in his pockets. He fished out enough to cover the ante, and figured he had enough to stay in for a few more hands. If things got out of control before he won a pot or two, he would be in for very few hands indeed.

Carter dealt out five cards to each player. The best Slocum could make of his hand was a pair of sixes and an ace, so when Eliza made a small bet, he called just like everyone else at the table. When they made their discards and got the replacements dealt to them, nobody seemed too excited. Slocum's hand didn't improve in the slightest, and a blind man could tell that Joey wasn't happy about the replacement for the one card he'd pitched. As for the others, Slocum couldn't hazard much of a guess.

"I'll bet," Eliza said. "Five dollars." She put her money in and gazed around as if she was expecting a round of applause.

Matt shrugged and threw in enough to cover the bet. "Why the hell not?" he grumbled.

Slocum knew he had the kid beat, but even he wouldn't have bet much of anything on a pair of sixes. Since the bet had been made and called by someone else before Carter had a chance to do anything, Slocum tossed his hand away.

"Too much for ya, huh?" Joey chided.

"Let's see your big move, kid," Slocum replied.

While Joey was anxious to puff his chest out and put on a show for the lady at the table, he lost his enthusiasm when he took a good look at the bad intentions written across Slocum's face. "I'm in," he announced meekly.

Carter wasn't impressed. "Then you'll need to be in for

ten more," he said as he tossed in the appropriate amount of chips.

Eliza stared at the pile of cash and chips in the middle of the table, and then looked at Carter. Putting on a playful scowl, she studied the man for a few more seconds before saying, "I think you're full of it, Mr. Carter."

Even though Carter's stony facade didn't crack, he did cock his head to one side and show her half of a calculated smirk. "One way to find out."

"I'm here to play," she said while looking at her cards for the third time in as many seconds. "Ten it is."

Matt let out a grunt and tossed his cards onto the pile of deadwood. "Way too much for a damned pair of fives," he said.

Slocum had been keeping an eye on Eliza throughout the entire game. When Matt folded, he saw the shadow of a twitch cross her face. The gesture was gone in an instant, but Slocum knew damn well Matt's fives were probably better than the old man thought.

Joey's sighing and deliberations were obvious posturing, and he buckled under the raise just like everyone at the table would have guessed. When it came time for Carter to act, he kept his eyes on Eliza and laid his cards down for all to see.

"Pair of queens," Carter announced.

Sighing heavily, Eliza spread out every single one of her cards. The only ones that went together were the four of hearts and the four of diamonds. "I almost had a straight," she pouted.

Carter leaned forward to rake in the pot. "You sure did. I just got lucky is all."

Eliza shrugged and sifted through the rest of the money she'd set upon the table. Nodding to herself, she placed her hands flat upon the felt surface and waited for the deck to be placed in front of her. After that, she shuffled the cards quickly and dealt them out.

Slocum looked around at the other players, but didn't really know what he was looking for. It was obvious that Eliza had done a good job of quickly charming every one of the men at the table. Even as she dealt the cards, she talked to them until she was comfortable enough to add a joke of her own into the ones being tossed back and forth between Matt and Joey.

The kid had some good lies to tell, but they weren't funny enough to make Slocum feel good about the round of crap he'd been dealt. Once more, he was stuck with a pair of sixes and three mismatched pieces of junk. He wondered if Eliza had dealt him an identical hand on purpose, but dismissed that thought when he realized that she hadn't dealt the first hand and didn't even know what he'd had in the first place. Maybe the sixes were just luck's way of convincing him that it did exist after all.

The betting went about the same as the first time. Matt threw in a small amount and Slocum matched it. Joey tried to hide a grin and bumped the bet up a bit. Carter matched the raise and Eliza did the same. She seemed a bit more at ease when she dealt out the cards to fill what the others threw away. Matt asked for two cards. Slocum took three. The kid was obviously chasing some more big game and only took one. Carter took three and Eliza only tossed one of her original five cards away.

"All right," Matt said. "Ten dollars should get this ball rolling."

At the start of the hand, Slocum's hand looked like a mess. When two of his three replacement cards wound up being kings, his prospects took a definite turn for the better. "Ten and five more," he said.

"Damn it!" Joey snapped as he flung his cards toward the deadwood piled next to Eliza's hand.

"I take it he's out," Carter said dryly. "I am, too."

"Not me," Eliza replied. Although she'd sounded pretty sure of herself, she dimmed a bit after looking through her money.

"If you want to bump it up," Matt told her, "I'll accept a line of credit."

"I'd better pace myself," she said. "I call."

Wearing a smile that was cautious but optimistic, Matt looked over at Slocum and asked, "How much more have you got?"

"Depends on how much you want to raise," Slocum replied.

Knowing he wasn't going to get much more out of Slocum than that, Matt grabbed some of the folded bills that were wedged in behind his small stack of chips. "How's twenty grab ya?"

Slocum thought he should bump up the bet a little more, but couldn't tell for certain whether he'd be milking the others for a bigger payout or playing into some sort of trap. The more he thought about it, the more possibilities drifted through his brain. After another second or two, he knew the other players were taking notes of how long he was taking time to think and probably reading plenty out of it. Rather than try to sift through more statistical nonsense, Slocum threw twenty dollars into the pot. Seeing as how that came close to the bottom of his bankroll anyhow, his previous deliberation seemed downright pointless.

Eliza looked over her cards again and then calmly put her money into the pot.

Now that the money was square, Matt proudly displayed his two pair. Deuces and tens. "What about it, John?" he asked. Can you beat that?"

"Yeah," Slocum replied as he showed his kings and sixes. "I think so."

"Aw, shit on a pile!" Matt said good-naturedly. "I thought I had you dead to rights."

"You did, until the last second," Slocum admitted. Before he reached for the pot, he looked across the table at Eliza. "How about you?"

She sighed and reluctantly showed a pair of jacks. "Everyone bet with less than that last time," she said. "I thought I stood a chance."

"Ol' Johnny boy just got lucky. Damn lucky!" Matt said. "Luck like that don't last."

Slocum pulled in his winnings and nodded to the older man beside him. "You got that right."

Before Slocum could get his money and chips stacked, the next hand was dealt. Since Matt was doing the dealing, Slocum had to get his thoughts together and decide what to do with his seven high. That choice was fairly easy to make, so he threw in a small bet and hoped for the best.

"Oh, I see that." Joey chuckled. "And another ten dollars!"

"Rein it in, kid," Carter growled.

Staring at his hand as if he'd just gotten a peek down the front of Eliza's dress, Joey replied, "You get a hand as good as this one and then you can talk."

"You don't have shit and everyone knows it." Without looking to see how Joey handled the observation, Carter shifted his eyes over to Eliza. He grinned and doubled the bet.

"All right," Eliza said with a tight smile of her own. "I'm in."

"What the hell," Matt said. "Might as well see if some of John's luck rubbed off on me." With that, he pushed in the proper amount of chips and looked at Slocum.

The thought crossed Slocum's mind to make his decision look like a tough one, but there wasn't any need to put on a show. He pitched his cards and leaned back in his chair to watch the sparks fly.

Joey came to a different conclusion. He decided to work up some drama by making it look like he was trying to decide which of his own children needed to be sacrificed to a raging sea.

"Fold or call," Carter snapped. "It's not that hard."

While he plainly wanted to do something else, Joey set his cards facedown in front of him. "Fold."

"All right then," Carter said. "Give me one card, Matt."

Matt obliged and then waited to hear from Eliza.

"Two for me," she said pleasantly.

Peeling a few cards from the deck, Matt announced, "Dealer takes three. And," he added while shooting Slocum a stern glare, "they'd better be good."

Carter was first to act and he had yet to take his eyes off Eliza. Even though she was a hell of a sight with her back straight and her figure wrapped up tightly in her laced corset, Eliza's feminine charms didn't seem to be what captivated Carter's attention. He watched her face and focused upon her eyes without so much as glancing down any farther.

"Fifty," Carter said as he pushed in a portion of his chips.

After looking at her cards and meeting Carter's gaze, Eliza shoved in a portion of cash. "Make it a hundred," she said.

Matt's eyebrows raised and he glanced down at what he'd been dealt. When he looked down again, the kid across from him remarked, "They ain't gonna change by you lookin' at them so much."

Although Slocum had already had his fill of the young man's talk, Matt took it in stride. The older fellow looked once more, shrugged, and said, "I suppose you're right, kid." He set his cards on top of the discard pile and waggled a finger at Slocum. "Made it longer than you, though."

"You sure did," Slocum chuckled. "Lost more than me, too."

"Wiseass."

Matt, Slocum, and even Joey laughed at the exchange.

Carter and Eliza, on the other hand, were too wrapped up in their own business to take part in the festivities.

Rubbing a finger along his chin, Carter finally let his eyes wander down the line of Eliza's neck and to the swell of her breasts. He kept his eyes moving until he was looking down at the stack of money and chips in front of him. "Two hundred," he said as he shoved in one of his stacks.

Eliza looked at her cards, pulled in a breath, and then pushed just about all of her money into the middle of the table. "That's your two hundred plus another two."

Slocum was the one to flinch this time. He'd seen plenty more money than that cross over a poker table, but he just hadn't been aware that Eliza had put that much money down when she'd started playing. When he looked at her money even closer, he could see that she still had at least another hundred and fifty left out in the open. Since Carter eyed that money the way a wolf eyed a bared throat, it seemed likely that he'd already gotten an accurate count and had even appraised the jewelry Eliza wore.

"You start off with three of a kind?" Carter asked. "Or did you get lucky on the draw?"

After checking her cards quickly, Eliza shrugged her shoulders and looked at Carter in a way that would have made any hungry wolf think twice about coming in for the kill. "One good way to find out," she replied.

Matt let out a low whistle and Joey started hooting up a storm. "She's got you there!" the young man said.

Carter's eyes snapped to the younger man. "Shut the fuck up, boy. You want to talk, then you'd best stop folding so goddamn much."

Slocum eased his hand down to rest upon his holster. Keeping his eyes on the rest of the table, he slipped the leather thong away from the hammer of the Colt Navy to make sure the six-shooter was clear for a fast draw.

Still wearing the snarl he'd shown to Joey, Carter let out a breath and shifted his focus to Eliza. He found her sitting with her back straight and the same confident expression that had been there before. As if to test her resolve a bit more, Carter leaned back and lowered one hand toward his gun belt.

"Easy, mister," Slocum warned.

When Carter looked over to see that Slocum had already gotten to his gun, his eyes flashed with an angry fire. Neither man had drawn their weapon just yet, but it was clearly only a matter of time before the smoke wagons started rolling.

Matt rapped his knuckles against the table and spoke in a sharp tone that caught everyone's ear. "Enough! Both of you. This is a friendly game, remember?"

Slocum's hand didn't budge. "No need to tell me," he said through gritted teeth. "I think he needs the reminder."

"Nothin's wrong with my memory," Carter said.

"Then get your hand back to your cards before I cash you out for good."

Considering how long he kept the fire in his eyes burning, Carter had clearly won more than his share of staring contests. Unlike those other times, the man in front of him didn't back down. In fact, the longer Carter insisted on testing him, the more Slocum looked like he was about to put him into a shallow grave.

"All right, all right," Carter said as he brought up his hand and showed it to Slocum. "It's a friendly game. What was the bet, Eliza?"

"I raised you two hundred," she replied while casting a quick glance in Slocum's direction.

Carter's eyes snapped back and forth between her and Slocum. Twitching as if he'd caught the tip of his tongue between his teeth, he tossed his cards over to the deadwood pile. Matt placed his hand over all the discards as if he was giving those cards their last rites.

"You got your three of a kind," Carter said. "You had me beat. Nice hand."

As she leaned forward to claim her winnings, Eliza replied, "Just as nice as the rest of me."

Finally allowing himself to relax, Carter nodded and leaned back into his chair.

"Hooo-wee, I'll just bet it's nice," Joey said.

Without even looking at the younger man, Carter growled, "Shut up, boy."

Joey wasn't happy about being put in his place, but he wasn't about to stand up to the man who'd done it. The next hand was fairly quiet, with Carter folding early and Matt winning with a pair of aces. As more hands were played, Slocum won once more, and wound up losing almost enough to bring him back down to where he'd started. The talk around the table gained steam quickly until everyone was laughing and joking.

Slocum kept his eye on Carter, but all that got him was a good view as the other man tried to gain ground with Eliza.

She batted her eyelashes right back at Carter, and even managed to look pretty when she lost.

"Don't fret, pretty lady," Carter said as he pulled in a pot. "After this game, I can take you out for a nice dinner. I only won enough for you and me, though. Your friend will have to fend for himself."

"Why don't I come back later when I'm hungry?" she said as she pushed her chair back from the table.

Slocum did the same and stood up as she did. The rest of the table got up as well, if only to be polite to Eliza.

"Been a pleasure playin' cards with ya, John," Matt said as he shook Slocum's hand. "You'd be real dangerous if you ever got a talent for lyin'."

"Practice makes perfect, I suppose," Slocum replied.

"True enough."

Joey spouted off a halfhearted farewell, but was more interested in winning some of his money back. Carter took in an eyeful of Eliza before returning to his own seat.

As Eliza cashed in her chips and walked out of Aunty Mae's, Slocum followed along behind her. The place was nice enough and the folks inside seemed friendly, but he still wasn't about to turn his back to a room full of gamblers.

7

Once she was out of Aunty Mae's, Eliza practically skipped across the street. After she'd gotten to the opposite board-walk, she spun around on the balls of her feet with more than enough speed to make her skirts swirl out around her.

"Well?" she asked expectantly. "What did you think?"

"It was fun," Slocum replied. "I haven't played poker for a while."

"That's not what I meant. I meant what did you think about how we did? We make a hell of a team!"

Slocum stepped up beside her and then turned to look back at Aunty Mae's. There wasn't anything particularly special about the place that hadn't been there before, so he glanced up and down the street. He wasn't sure what he was supposed to see, but Slocum sure felt like he was missing something. Finally, he looked back at Eliza and shrugged. "We were a team?" he asked.

She scowled a bit and swatted his shoulder. "Of course we were! The beautiful part is that we looked like a team walking up to that table and we still managed to do well."

"Perhaps you should explain it to me then."

Eliza started walking along the side of the street and wrapped her arm around Slocum's so she could drag him with her. She lowered her voice so she wasn't shouting, but she still seemed excited. "When two people walk up to a game like we did, any gambler's going to suspect they're partners trying to run some sort of dodge. We didn't do anything too suspicious, so they probably just figured you were my protection or possibly just a friend."

"That's what we told them," Slocum said.

"Yes, but what matters is what they thought. Just having you there was enough to put them on their best behavior as far as I was concerned." Waving her free hand as if she'd suddenly become exasperated, Eliza explained, "There's a lot to think about, but the important thing is that I was able to use everything to my advantage. Having you there, the way those men reacted to me, the way they reacted to you, the way those fellows took turns trying to get on my good side . . ."

"Now, I did spot that," Slocum said.

Eliza smiled and tightened her grip around his arm. "All of that went a long way for me to get a read on them. Especially that hand where you and Carter almost got rough."

Slocum nodded. "He was suspecting something or just getting flustered. Either way, that almost turned real bad real quick."

"But it didn't!" Eliza said proudly. "That's because we were both working well together."

"I was just sitting there. I barely even won anything."

"You weren't supposed to win. That was my job. Your job was to back me up if things went bad, or keep things from getting bad at all."

Slocum shook his head. The more Eliza chattered, the more he felt like there was a horsefly rattling around inside his ears. "You walked over and started playing. I just sat down and did the same."

"You backed me up, John. Do you know I've worked with men who would have turned things against me at the first opportunity?"

"I wouldn't exactly know how to do that," Slocum admitted.

"That's fine, but there's also plenty of men who would

have backed down when Carter started getting riled. Some men could have jumped the gun and turned that game into a shooting match, but you were perfect, John. Perfect!"

Shrugging and accepting the praise coming his way, Slocum steered them both around the next corner so they could head toward Second Street. "All right. So you were testing me."

Eliza nodded. "And you passed."

"I thought you were going to show me a thing or two. You made it seem like you were going to prove what a good partner you could be, not the other way around."

"I won, didn't I?"

"How much?"

Keeping her eyes on the street in front of her, Eliza said, "I tripled my money."

Slocum stopped dead in his tracks. "The hell you did!"

After disentangling herself from around Slocum's arm, Eliza reached into a pocket that was well hidden among the folds of her skirt. When she pulled her hand from that pocket, she fanned out the money she'd gotten when she'd cashed out of Aunty Mae's. "Triple," she reported. "And then some."

Snatching the money from her hand, Slocum flipped through it to count it up. He hadn't known exactly how much Eliza had started with, but there was upward of a thousand dollars now. "Where did you get all of this?" he asked.

"You were sitting right there, John."

"I know. The biggest pot I saw you win was when Carter almost drew his gun."

"That's right. The rest was won throughout the other hands. A hundred or two here, another couple hundred there . . ."

"But I saw you lose, too!"

Since there were some people walking down the street toward them, Eliza folded up the money and tucked it away. She took Slocum's arm and started walking down the street again. "I lost some, but won more. That's how you win at any game," she said. "In poker, you try for the big pots, but you make most of your money chipping away slowly at the others at the table."

"That makes sense and I *was* watching, but . . ." Now that Slocum thought back on it, he could recall several more of those pots growing to pretty good sizes before Eliza raked them in. Finally, he had to admit one thing. "You're really good, Eliza."

"Thank you."

"I figured you came out ahead, but not by that much."

"Chipping away," Eliza repeated.

"Were you cheating?"

She shook her head and told him, "No. Not even a little."

"But you have cheated at the card table."

"What makes you say that?"

"Because," Slocum replied, "you didn't look offended when I asked the question."

"Everyone cheats, John. I've dabbled here and there, but I don't always have someone watching out for me. Don't get any ideas, though. I can handle myself, but I'd rather not take those chances when it's just me and a room full of men out to prove themselves."

"I understand that more than just about anything else you've said after leaving that place." They both had a laugh at that, but there was something else that Slocum wanted to know. "You didn't even cheat on that hand where Carter got all riled up?"

Shaking her head, Eliza was proud to tell him, "Nope. Not even then. That would have been the perfect time to pull something, but even he knew that much and was watching for it."

"So you just happened to get some good cards?"

"Nope."

Slocum grinned and asked, "What did you have?"

The smirk on Eliza's face was playful and devilish at the same time. "I was going for a flush, but didn't get it."

"So you had nothing?"

"That's right."

"I thought you had at least a pair or probably even three of a kind."

"I know," Eliza said. "That's what Carter thought, too. In fact, he was sure of it."

"You think so?"

"Did you notice how I looked at my cards when I had a good hand?"

Slocum thought back to the game and did recall a few times when she'd glanced down more than once. "I suppose so," he told her.

"Well, Carter and Matt noticed it. I'm not sure about the kid. I suspect Joey was being fleeced by the other two when we arrived. That kid had too much money and Carter seemed too bent out of shape when we came along to step on their toes. They perked up just fine once I showed them a few little flinches here and sly grins there. I gave them just enough to make them think they had a read on me."

"And I suppose you were getting a read on them," Slocum said.

When Eliza shrugged, it was the first time in the last few minutes that she hadn't seemed to be completely happy with herself. "Yes and no. I think I might have picked up a few things, but they could have been nothing. If we were there longer, I would have gotten plenty!" she explained. "I was trying to catch your attention so you'd know I was going in for the kill."

"You were?" Slocum asked. "You mean when Carter was getting upset?"

"Yes. Didn't you see me signaling to you?"

"Not really."

"Oh. Well, we'll have to work on that. I mean, we can work it out if you still want to be partners and all."

Slocum didn't mind playing poker. He didn't mind gambling as such. He preferred to earn his keep through honest work, but he didn't cotton much to the notion of someone else gambling with his wages. There were too many things that could go wrong where he would still be pulling his end and somehow not getting paid. Then again, flat out refusing Eliza when she was watching him expectantly was easier said than done.

"You do know how to work a poker game, I give you that much."

Hearing that was enough to make Eliza beam. "Thank you very much," she said as if she was accepting applause from an audience.

"But I won't be part of some team that runs con games or sets up some sort of double-dealing scheme. Card cheats are damn thieves and they tend to get strung up or shot down when they're caught. You ask me, most of them are getting what they deserve."

Eliza was quick to shake her head. "I've cheated before and I know how a lot of it is done, but it's too dangerous to be anything but a last resort. There's plenty of other ways to win that aren't as messy as shaving cards or stuffing aces up your sleeves. I wanted you to sit in on that game so you could see what I was talking about."

The thought of playing second fiddle to a card cheat didn't set well at all with Slocum, and it showed by the scowl on his face. After what he'd seen during the game and heard afterward, he had to admit one thing. "That was damn impressive."

"And that was just a few quick hands," Eliza said. "It only gets better once I have some time to get to know the people I'm playing with and let them think they've gotten to know me."

"What about Armand Theil?" Slocum asked. "I suppose he's gotten to know you pretty well."

Some of the light in Eliza's eyes dimmed with the mention of that name. "He thinks I cheated him, but all I did was turn things to my advantage. You saw me play. Sometimes, someone at the table might think they're being swayed one way or another but they just can't put their finger on it. More often than not, they realize it before it's too late to do anything about it. Most of the time, they pitch a fit and try to get their money back."

"And other times they chase you out of town," Slocum pointed out.

"Or across two states through Lord knows how many territories. I won't allow myself to be hunted, John. I can't live that way."

"You may just die that way."

"Maybe," she replied without hesitation. "But I'd rather die that way than go on running from that man. If I beat him at his own game when he's got all his men to back him up, he'll lose his steam and give up on chasing me."

"You certain about that?" Slocum asked.

"I'm betting my life on it."

"If I come in with you, it's not just *your* life."

When she smiled this time around, Eliza looked as if she barely had the strength to lift her head up. "You're the gunfighter. Not me. You'll handle yourself just fine or you'll at least know when it's time to run."

Slocum's eyes darted toward one of the many figures moving along the street. There was something about that figure that caught his attention. Since the figure ducked into an alley a split second before Slocum could get a better look, it was obvious that the man didn't want to be seen.

"It's time to move along right now," Slocum said.

The spark in Eliza's eyes was nearly snuffed out when she heard that. "Oh, well, that's your choice I suppose."

"Both of us need to move along," Slocum said as he grabbed her arm and pulled her along. "Someone's watching us."

"Who? Where?"

They were at the end of one street and about to turn onto another. Because of that, Slocum knew he could circle around and close in on the man before he got too far away.

"John, tell me who you saw!"

Keeping his expression calm, Slocum stopped at the mouth of an alley and turned so he could keep his eye on

Eliza while still being able to spot movement from the edge of his line of sight. "Someone ducked into an alley back there," he told her. "If they're following us, they'll probably show up in this alley right here."

Eliza reflexively looked in that direction, but Slocum shook her once to force her to look at him.

"This is the sort of thing I'm best at," he explained. "If you want me to work for you, you'll need to do what I say when I say it. Understand?"

She nodded and kept quiet. Her expression showed that she was more excited than scared by the sudden turn of events.

Before Slocum could say another word, he caught a hint of motion from the alley. He thought he could hear something rustling in that direction, but he couldn't be certain the sound wasn't just a horse dragging its feet or a wagon wheel with a peculiar squeak.

"When I let go of your arm, I want you to run past me and duck into that store across the street."

Eliza nodded quickly.

Even though Slocum kept his face pointed at her, he was actually looking in every other direction. He didn't pay any mind to the flush in her cheeks or the way her quick breaths made her bosom swell against the confines of her clothing. Every noise she heard caused her to twitch reflexively in that direction. The longer she waited in silence, the more expectant she became for the hammer to drop.

Slocum was more interested in the horses slowly plodding down the street and the flow of people near the storefront on the other side. He didn't have to wait long before there were enough people on the other side of the street to hide Eliza once she got there. As soon as he let go of her arm, Eliza darted across the street like an arrow that had been loosed from a bow.

Turning toward the bit of movement he'd spotted, Slocum placed himself between the alley and the path Eliza needed to take to cross the street. Sure enough, there was someone skulking in the alley. Judging by the way he hunkered down and rushed to retrace his steps away from the street, that person wasn't anxious to be caught.

Slocum set his eyes upon his target and took off running.

The two buildings that formed the alley were short and close together. Slocum had to jump over a few piles of trash and turn his body sideways to maneuver through the cramped quarters, but so did anyone else that was rushing through the narrow space.

The man had a head start on Slocum, but didn't have many options on where to go after he'd been spotted. Once he reached the end of one alley, he made a sharp left and ducked into another alley that led back to Aunty Mae's. Slocum knocked over a few crates and cracked his shoulder against a wall, but he was able to charge forward and gain some ground. A few more lunging steps followed by a strong jump put him close enough to grab hold of the man's jacket.

Slocum made a fist around the man's collar and pulled. The man squirmed and kicked like a wild animal. He nearly wriggled out of his jacket altogether, but Slocum was able to end the struggle with a hard knee to the small of the man's back. As soon as the man began to go limp, Slocum knocked his legs out from under him and slammed him face-first to the ground.

The sight of the man's long, greasy hair was enough to give Slocum a good idea of who the man was. Now that he was close enough to see the fellow's face, he grabbed some of that hair and twisted his head around to look through the spectacles covering the man's eyes.

"Not so tough without your shotgun, Lem?" Slocum asked.

Lem was a wiry cuss and kept struggling to get free of Slocum, even when his efforts caused some of his own hair to rip loose from his scalp. After taking a second blow from Slocum's knee against his back, Lem twisted around to look over his shoulder. "Let me up and we'll see how tough I am!"

"Maybe later. First, you get to answer a few questions."

"The answer to all yer goddamn questions is FUCK YOUR—"

The rest of Lem's tirade was cut short when Slocum pounded Lem's face against the ground. Lem's muffled voice mixed in with the sounds of cracking glass and gravel grinding into flesh.

Slocum looked up to find an older man at the mouth of the alley looking in on the scene with startled confusion. "He's drunk and ornery," Slocum explained.

That was good enough for the old man, who shrugged and continued along his way.

Taking hold of Lem's hair with his left hand, Slocum drew his shooting iron and pressed its barrel against the back of Lem's head. "Look here, you cocksucker. The only reason you're still alive right now is because you did the smart thing and ran instead of taking a shot at me."

"We ain't after you!" Lem moaned through a bloody mouth.

"Like coming after a woman makes things a whole lot better."

"She's a damn cheater!"

"You scared her out of her mind," Slocum said. "She's on the run and being shot at by the likes of you. That makes you even for any gambling losses, cheating or otherwise. You hear me?"

"But she took—"

After slamming Lem's face against the ground once more, Slocum growled, "You're even! Understand?" Rather than wait for Lem to come up with more words of his own, Slocum moved Lem's head up and down. "Good. Glad to see you agree with me."

Slocum opened his fist and let Lem's head fall forward. He kept the Colt aimed at the man as he stood up and dusted himself off a bit. "I meant to deliver this message to you in a more civil manner, but you forced the issue by lurking in alleyways and shooting through windows. Eliza Banner is to be left alone. Deliver that message to whoever hired you because if I have to send another one, it won't be so nice."

Pulling himself up, Lem used the back of one hand to clean off his face, while keeping the other on the ground for support. "Oh, I will. You wanna tell me who the hell you are? That way we'll know what to write on yer grave marker."

Slocum turned, aimed, and fired in one smooth motion. The Colt Navy barked once and sent its bullet into the ground between Lem's fingers. "I'm the man that'll be keeping an eye on Miss Banner. That's all you need to know."

8

Eliza was waiting for Slocum in front of the store where he'd told her to go. The moment she spotted him crossing the street, she rushed over to him and asked, "What happened? I heard a shot."

"It was nothing," Slocum replied. "Just a little misunderstanding with one of Theil's men."

"Is he . . . I mean . . . did you . . . ?"

"A misunderstanding," he assured her. "Nobody's hurt and I'm sure he understands that attacking you isn't such a good idea anymore."

She smiled and wrapped her arm once more around Slocum's. Both of them continued walking toward the corner, but Eliza pulled Slocum in the other direction when he began heading for the stable. "Not that way," she said calmly. "There was some folks in a tizzy over there and I think one of them was a law dog."

Slocum took a look over there for himself. The upset locals were easy enough to spot. They were waving their arms and pointing toward the alley where Lem had been put down. There was more than enough sunlight to glint off the tin on a younger man's shirt, which convinced Slocum to take heed of Eliza's advice. "Good eye," he said.

"I take it you've accepted my offer?"

"We're partners."

"Right. Think of it as a business venture." Raising her other hand to show him a wad of folded money, she reached over to slip it into Slocum's shirt pocket. "Here's your first payment. It's a cut of the winnings from that game at Aunty Mae's."

"How much?"

"If you want to count it . . ."

"No," Slocum cut in. "That's not exactly what I was after."

She picked up on his meaning right away and said, "It's fifty percent. Since you're my only partner at the moment, that's as fair as I can be."

"You'll throw in for the traveling expenses as well."

"Of course."

Slocum pulled the arm she was holding onto closer to his side and then patted her hand. "Sounds like a real good arrangement. At least for the moment. Were you planning on taking on any more partners?"

"That depends."

"On what?"

"On how well you pull your share of the load," Eliza replied with a playful shrug. "I might just have to hire someone else on if you get lazy."

"Lazy, huh?" Slocum asked. "Since I'm so lazy, why don't you carry your own bags and load them onto the horses?"

"I was just kidding, John."

"Really? I wasn't."

To Eliza's credit, she hauled all of her things to the stable and seemed ready to saddle up her horse and get everything loaded onto its back without any help. Then again, she could very well have simply been calling Slocum's bluff. Either way, they were both in their saddles and riding out of East Padre by early evening.

Slocum had intended on leaving town a bit earlier, but the poker game had chewed up a good amount of the day. It was more than worth the loss of miles that could have been covered in that time, since Slocum was fairly confident that backing Eliza was a good move in more than one respect.

First of all, she was a hell of a gambler. What he'd seen, coupled with what she described while they rode, was enough to convince him that she knew what she was doing when it came to poker. Whether or not he could fully trust her was another matter. Gamblers, after all, were the sort of folks who were always looking for new angles. And once a gambler learned how to cheat, they tended to use that knowledge every so often.

Secondly, his time with Eliza had proven that she was in some serious trouble. The gunmen that were coming after her meant business. The three that Theil had hired might not have been the deadliest to have crossed Slocum's path, but they were sure persistent and they didn't seem ready to stop anytime soon.

The terrain outside of East Padre was high and rocky. Glancing up at the jagged peaks overlooking the trail was enough to give Slocum visions of ambushes coming down at them from any number of directions. It wouldn't take much more than a single man and a rifle to put either of the two riders into a whole world of hurt. Since firing a shot from cover seemed about right for the likes of Lem or the other two gunmen, Slocum snapped his reins to get his horse moving at a quicker pace.

Eliza followed along, and even rushed ahead of him a bit. When she looked back over her shoulder, the challenge in her eyes was unmistakable. "How much faith do you have in that horse of yours?" she asked.

Slocum rushed past her and replied, "Don't know. I haven't put him through his paces yet."

"I know a real good way to test him. How about a race?"

"Anything to take some more of your money," he replied as he tapped his heels against his horse's sides.

It seemed Slocum's horse was as anxious to get moving as he was. It broke into a run and kicked up a cloud of dust behind its churning hooves.

Eliza leaned down closer to her horse's neck and tightened her grip upon her reins. She even let out a few yelps to move her horse along.

Although Slocum's first instinct was to try and win the race, he reminded himself of what they were doing and he subtly pulled back on the reins. His right hand drifted toward the cross-draw holster around his waist and he let his eyes wander among the crooked, rocky lines of his surroundings.

If someone had managed to get into a proper ambush spot, they would most likely stick their necks out when they had a clean shot. Slocum figured the horses were moving fast enough to keep Eliza relatively safe. If one of Theil's men was good enough to make that shot, they could pick them off at any time no matter what Slocum did.

It could have been a risky gamble.

Theil might have had a hell of a good marksman on his payroll.

The ambushers might have already gotten out of pistol range and set up a shot.

Eliza's horse could trip over a loose rock.

Lightning could strike them both dead on the spot.

There were always things that could go wrong.

This time, none of them did.

Eliza was right. She was lucky after all.

Unable to spot so much as a clump of tumbleweed moving alongside the trail, Slocum snapped his reins and overtook Eliza's horse. The two of them traded positions for a few more miles before their horses started wheezing under the constant strain. Rather than push the animals any further, they called it a draw and allowed both animals to slow to a more comfortable pace. As the day had worn on, Eliza had unbuttoned her blouse a bit more so she could cool herself off. Although a bit of sweat had beaded upon her skin, Slocum noticed she always waited until he was looking at her before pulling another button free and fanning her newly bared skin. When she did catch him looking, she always grinned and let her hand wander down along herself before finally easing it away.

With the sun on its way down, there was no difficulty in keeping their noses pointed westward. Even though East Padre wasn't too far from the border of Arizona Territory, Slocum knew they wouldn't make it out of New Mexico before it became too dark to ride. The weather had been cooperating thus far, but there were some clouds rolling in from the north. A good amount of stars would be blotted out and there was only a sliver of moon due to show itself that evening.

The darkness would become thick as smoke in a brushfire before too long. Riding too fast in those conditions could prove more harmful that any rifleman's bullet.

Slocum allowed the horses to walk for a while longer before giving them one last run for the day. After that, he steered toward an outcropping of rocks to the south.

"We'll camp there for the night," Slocum said.

Looking in the direction he'd pointed, Eliza asked, "Isn't that a bit off course? We could just head due west and cut our ride down a bit."

"I don't think anyone's following us, but I don't want to take any chances. Weaving every now and then along the way makes it easier for me to see if we picked up a tail, and harder for anyone to guess our route so they can ride ahead and settle in for an ambush."

"All right. Just as long as you know what you're doing."

"What's the matter?" Slocum asked as he looked over to her. "Don't you trust me to do my part?"

"Sure." After nodding and settling into her saddle once more, she spoke with some more confidence in her voice. "I mean . . . of course I do."

That was good enough for now. The rest would just have to wait until they got through Navajo country.

"Indians?" Eliza asked. "Are you sure?"

Slocum carried another armload of branches he'd gathered from the immediate area surrounding the spot he'd chosen to make camp. The horses were tied off to a dead log, content to graze among a few patches of grass that had managed to poke up through the hard-packed ground. Dumping the wood next to the sputtering fire they'd built, Slocum replied, "Pretty sure. I've been through this stretch of land more than once. That's how I knew about this spot."

Lowering her voice to a grumble, Eliza said, "Then maybe you could have picked a spot without any Indians."

"Good luck finding a spot like that where we're going. We're just two riders without any wagons. There's really no good reason for the Navajo to give us any trouble."

"What about other tribes?"

Slocum hunkered down next to the fire and looked around as if he could spot all the different factions of redskins. Shrugging, he said, "Sure. There could be plenty of other tribes about. There could be scouting parties, hunting parties, even raiding parties, and they may or may not be affiliated with any tribe at all."

After shifting her head around to look in any and every direction she could, Eliza settled her gaze back upon Slocum. "You're fooling with me."

Slocum looked around in almost the same way as Eliza had. When he looked back at her, he wore a concerned expression on his face that lasted for about three seconds before it cracked into a smile. "Maybe I am fooling a little."

Eliza reached out to smack Slocum's shoulder with almost enough force to push him over. "That was not funny, John Slocum!"

"I don't know. I thought it was pretty damn funny."

"So there really aren't any Indians around here?"

"Oh, there are Indians all right. I just don't think we should have anything to worry about. I'm making sure to steer clear of the spots where they don't want outsiders to be. Since we won't be starting any trouble with them, they should leave us alone."

Still looking at him as if she was expecting more laughter, Eliza soon began to lose her smile. "But they are around?"

"Yes. It's open country, Eliza. There could also be bandits, snakes, and just about anything else, but I wouldn't lose sleep over it. So long as we keep our eyes open, we should be just fine. It's the same with walking through a town or crossing a river."

"I suppose so," she replied. "It's just been a while since I've traveled this way."

"I've found that you come across more snakes in town than you do around a campfire."

"Don't forget poker tables. Snakes love slithering around poker tables."

Even though they were both talking about snakes of the two-legged variety, Slocum didn't have trouble picturing any number of gamblers with forked tongues flicking from their mouths. In fact, the picture seemed rather appropriate.

"You hungry?" Slocum asked.

"Starved."

"I know you're used to town food, but we don't have much choice out here."

"There were a few jackrabbits over there," Eliza said as she nodded into the distance. "Maybe you could impress me with your gun-handling skills and get us some fresh meat along the way?"

Slocum didn't even bother looking toward the stretch of ground where Eliza had seen the jackrabbits. "Maybe I can impress you some other time. I'd rather not make all that noise."

"You think those Indians will get the wrong idea if they heard shots?"

"You don't need to fret so much about Indians. I already told you. In case you forgot, there are some other killers that may be coming after us."

Stretching her legs as she followed Slocum over to where he'd dropped the saddlebags, Eliza let out half a laugh. "Those idiots are probably already lost. Either that or they rode on ahead to meet up with Theil."

"Do you know that for certain?" Slocum asked.

"Well . . . no."

"Then tonight we'll stay quiet and see what we can see. Fortunately, from this spot we can see an awful lot."

"Won't they be able to see us?"

"Which is why we've got such a sorry excuse for a campfire," Slocum told her. The fire he'd built was large enough to provide some warmth and warm a bit of food, but not nearly enough to catch someone's attention from miles away. That story could change if someone was hunting them down and knew where to look, but Slocum wasn't exactly opposed to that either.

It would make things a little easier for him if Dawes, Lem, and Mark did try to make a run at them that night. Slocum's eyes were used to the darkness enough for him to spot a man approaching camp, and he was confident he could hear horses approaching as well. Just to be certain, he'd scattered a good portion of branches around the campsite when he'd been gathering wood for the fire. If someone did manage to get close without Slocum seeing them, they'd surely step on one of those branches or make some noise while clearing a path.

Since it wouldn't do Eliza any good to worry about all of that, Slocum let the matter slide. She seemed to have other things on her mind anyway.

After taking a few cans from his saddlebag, Slocum went back to the fire and sat down. It wasn't long before Eliza scooted in beside him and got close enough for her shoulder to press against Slocum's arm.

"I haven't properly thanked you for saving my life," she said.

"You can thank me by opening this can of peaches."

Taking the can as well as the opener, Eliza eventually got the top bent back enough to get to the preserved fruit inside. Handing it back to him, she said, "That wasn't what I had in mind."

"I know, but that's the best we'll get tonight. I'm not shooting any rabbits."

"Actually, I was thinking more along the lines of building

up more of an appetite." With that, Eliza reached out to place one hand against the side of Slocum's face. She leaned in and kissed him gently upon the lips. After a few seconds, she leaned back again, but only far enough for their mouths to no longer be touching.

Slocum could feel the warmth from Eliza's body. Her lips had a sweet taste to them and when he looked into her eyes, he could see a promise for much more than just a kiss. As if sensing his thoughts, she parted her lips expectantly.

"If we're being followed," Slocum said quietly, "we could be attacked tonight."

"If we were being followed, wouldn't you have known about it already?" Eliza moved her hand along the front of Slocum's pants and then reached between his legs. "I want you," she whispered. "If you're worried about an ambush, I'll be real quiet." Her hand slid down a bit farther, allowing her to stroke his cock through the layer of denim until she felt it become hard. Working his erection even more, she said, "And if someone does take a shot at me, I can't think of anything else I'd rather be doing."

It went against every fiber of Slocum's being, but he resisted tearing off Eliza's clothes and throwing her onto his bedroll. "We need to be careful," he said as Eliza tugged at his belt and ran the tip of her tongue along his neck. "For tonight, we need to keep watch."

"All right then," she said as she stretched out on her back and bent her knees so her skirts fell away from the lower portion of her body. "You can watch." From there, she moved her hands along her own body and slipped them beneath her undergarments. When she touched the right spot between her legs, Eliza closed her eyes and let out a slow sigh.

Slocum's first instinct was to rip Eliza's dress off and throw it as far away as he could. The paltry light from the fire played along the exposed skin of her legs and thighs, making her sweat glitter in the combination of light from the flames and the stars. As he let his eyes wander, Slocum saw Eliza reach up with one hand to open the front of her dress.

"There," she said as she exposed her firm breasts. "That's what you want, isn't it?" She moved her fingers along her nipples, and even rubbed them until the pink, dime-sized patches of skin responded to her touch. She writhed on the ground and sighed again as she continued to tease the sensitive skin of her body.

The buttons along her dress came free, exposing the layers of simple cotton she'd worn for the day's ride. Now that she'd shifted the dress some more, Slocum could see the entire creamy slope of her legs as well as the downy hair between them.

"God, I want you, John. Come here."

Not one to refuse a lady, Slocum crawled over to her and straddled the leg that she'd flattened against the ground. She lifted that leg just enough to brush against the erection that was pressing uncomfortably against his jeans. The moment his hand touched the exposed skin of her leg, Slocum moved it upward until he got to the warmth between her thighs.

Her body was hot and the lips of her pussy were soft to the touch. When Slocum eased his fingers up and down along those lips, he felt a tremble work all the way through her body until Eliza was arching her back against the ground.

"Yes, John. That's it. That feels so good."

He knew it felt good. He could tell by the way Eliza became wetter and wetter the longer he rubbed her there. Grinning at how he was driving her so wild, Slocum waited until he thought she was going to start growling before slipping one of his fingers inside her. Eliza let out a moan, but quickly caught herself and quieted down again.

"Sorry," she whispered. "I couldn't help mys—"

Slocum took away her next words along with her next breath when he slipped two fingers inside her instead of just the one. All Eliza could do was grab hold of the ground with both hands and open her legs so Slocum could move his hand freely between them.

As much as he wanted to stick to his old plan, Slocum had gone too far to turn back now. He positioned himself between her legs so his mouth was only a few inches away from her pussy when he took his fingers out of her. The moment he pulled that hand away, he pressed his tongue between her wet lips.

Eliza lifted her butt off the ground and pushed herself against his mouth while somehow managing to keep quiet. Just as she was about to take hold of Slocum's hair, she felt his tongue suddenly pull out of her.

"What is it?" she gasped. "Why did you stop?"

"Did you hear that?"

"Hear what? Are you joking again? This isn't . . ." But she stopped herself short when she saw Slocum quickly raise his hand to silence her. She looked around, but could only see the shadows that were growing thicker around the camp. All she could hear was the faint rustle of some branches.

"Something's moving out there," Slocum whispered.

"It's probably just an animal. Or it could be the wind. It could be anything." She begged, "Just get back over here!"

Slocum was already on his feet. When he looked at Eliza, the fierce expression on his face was more than enough to silence her. "Stay right there and don't make a sound. I set out those branches to alert me if anyone was coming. If something's rustling through them, I'd be a fool to ignore it."

"But . . ."

"But nothing," he snapped. "Stay put and keep quiet."

Eliza pulled her skirts down and wrapped herself up in her clothing as if she was fit to be tied. The fire in her eyes was almost brighter than the fire crackling in the middle of the camp, and it only grew brighter as Slocum stalked away into the darkness.

There was plenty she wanted to say, but she kept from saying it.

9

There was plenty Slocum wanted to do, but he kept himself from doing it.

His blood rolled through his veins like kerosene that had been touched by a lit match. He could still smell Eliza when he pulled in his next breath, and he could still feel her wetness upon his fingers. There was an aching in his groin that made it seem like his own body was punishing him for not following through on what had been started.

He knew he'd been gruff with Eliza, but Slocum had to do whatever he needed to do in order to get away from that camp. Truth be told, it took every bit of strength he could muster to pull himself away from her when he'd heard that rustling.

It was a rustling, he had to admit, that could very well have been caused by the wind or an animal.

It could also have been from a skinny assassin crawling up to the camp to extract some revenge for the beating he'd taken in an alley not too long ago. Slocum had no trouble at all in picturing Lem sneaking up and taking his shots from the cover of darkness. In fact, the more Slocum thought about that, the more he became convinced that Lem would prefer that sort of fight. It would allow the sneaky little prick to get a show before putting a few well-placed shots into some unsuspecting backs.

Slocum gritted his teeth and kept thinking along those lines. It did him good to steel himself like that before a fight. It also helped take his mind away from what he was missing right about now.

It didn't take his mind too far away, but it helped.

Actually, it didn't help at all.

Keeping his head down and his steps light, Slocum grabbed the Winchester that lay beneath his saddle. After picking up his rifle, Slocum circled the camp and listened for another one of those sounds that had drawn him away.

Suddenly, he stopped.

There was as good a chance that he was closing in on an intruder as there was of that same intruder making some noise to draw him away from camp. The simple fact was that Slocum had to take his chances with what he was doing. It wasn't as though he could drag Eliza along with him and expect her to stay safe. No, Slocum had to keep going and hope she followed the simple orders he'd given her. If Eliza couldn't do that, she wouldn't last long no matter who helped her.

While those things rushed through Slocum's mind, he never stopped moving. The rifle was held at hip level. His eyes were narrowed into slits and his brow was furrowed with concentration.

There was somebody out there.

Slocum could feel it in his gut.

Turning on the balls of his feet while shifting so he could sweep his gaze past the camp, Slocum prepared himself for anything. When he spotted some movement, he brought the Winchester up to his shoulder and drew his finger taut against the trigger. Stopping short before firing a round, Slocum caught sight of the movement again . . . only to find Eliza sticking her head up for a moment to get a look around.

Since Slocum wasn't about to announce his position, he kept his mouth shut. Every part of him was practically screaming out at Eliza. He didn't make a peep, but the inside of Slocum's head was full of insistent, and not so polite, demands for Eliza to do as she'd been told and lay the hell down.

In a matter of seconds, Eliza flattened herself against the ground. Either she'd come to her senses or somehow heard Slocum cursing her out in his head, but she was down all the same.

Another rustle came from the shadows.

This time, the sound came from Slocum's left, which meant it was away from the camp. The only part of him that moved was his eyes as he twitched to get a look in that direction. His head followed and the rest of his body shifted slightly to point him toward the noise, making Slocum look like a bobcat that was stalking its prey.

He kept his upper body leaning slightly forward while hunkering down as low as he could. Slocum's legs alternated between stretching in one direction and curling up directly beneath his body. That way, he could move toward the source of the sound without letting his head raise up any higher than what was absolutely necessary. Slocum concentrated hard enough to hear the next batch of rustling when it drifted through the air. It was still coming from directly in front of him, so he picked up his pace to close some distance between himself and whoever was sneaking around the perimeter of the camp.

When Slocum got close enough to hear boots scraping against the dirt, he grinned to himself. Soon, he would be close enough to hear breathing, and after that it would be too late for the intruder in the shadows to do much of anything. Things couldn't have gone any better. That is, until Slocum's heel lowered upon one of the branches he'd set out earlier that night.

The snap of breaking wood was like a gunshot in Slocum's ears. He froze in his spot and held his breath, hoping that he hadn't spooked the intruder.

For a second, it seemed that the slip had gone unnoticed.

Then Slocum saw a slender shadow explode into motion as a figure gave up his hiding spot and broke into a run toward the camp.

Slocum waited a second before running after the figure, since it seemed that person was more interested in getting to Eliza. As soon as Slocum knew he was behind the person, he charged after the intruder at a dead run. The person was fast, but Slocum used every bit of steam he had to close in on him.

His legs ached and his muscles cried for mercy, but Slocum kept pushing. When he was close enough to see the back of the person's head, Slocum holstered his Colt and launched himself toward the man. Slocum reached out with both arms while in midair, stretching all the way out until even his fingertips felt the strain. Slocum's left hand scraped down along the man's back until his fingers snagged upon the back of the guy's belt. From there, the weight of Slocum's body hitting the ground was more than enough to bring the man down with him.

Slocum grunted as his chest hit the ground and a good portion of the wind was knocked from his lungs. The fellow kept his legs scrambling against the dirt, and let out a surprised yelp when he was brought down.

As Slocum gulped down a few quick breaths, he knew he wouldn't be able to pull in a good-sized breath for a little while. Therefore, it was pure determination that kept him moving forward while reeling the man in. Suddenly, the man twisted around and swung a hunting knife toward Slocum's face.

The blade sliced through the air with a vicious hiss. There was just enough light to glint off the sharpened steel as it moved along a deadly arc that would take it straight across the bridge of Slocum's nose. Even as he leaned back to avoid the incoming steel, Slocum kept his grip upon the man's belt. That instinct nearly proved to be costly as the blade nicked Slocum's nose before continuing along its course.

Still unsure as to how badly he'd been cut, Slocum moved

fast before he lost too much blood. He pulled on the man's belt and reached out to grab the guy's shirt. Just as Slocum got a grip on the intruder's sleeve, the man swung his knife back around toward Slocum.

This time, all Slocum needed to do was duck his head to clear a path for the incoming weapon. Slocum managed to avoid the knife, but the intruder's swing knocked the hat right off Slocum's head. As soon as he felt the swing pass over him, Slocum snapped his head up to get a look at the intruder.

To Slocum's surprise, the man wasn't Lem.

Even more of a surprise was that the man wasn't anyone Slocum recognized at all.

The intruder was a young man with a narrow jaw and close-cropped hair. The scars on his face and arms marked him as someone who'd had plenty of experience fighting with that knife of his. The fiery look in his eyes made it clear that he was more than ready to bury that blade deep into Slocum's gullet.

Now that he'd crawled forward a bit, Slocum was able to grab hold of the intruder's arm before he could swing his knife again. It wasn't a perfect grip, but was solid enough to buy Slocum another second or two. He used that time to scramble closer and then bury the elbow of his free arm into the intruder's stomach.

The intruder let out a pained grunt. The blow from Slocum's elbow took away enough of his steam to allow Slocum to pin his knife hand to the ground. From there, Slocum drove one knee into the man's chest and rained a few punches down onto the intruder's face.

"Who the hell are you?" Slocum asked after he'd felt the satisfying crunch of nose cartilage against his fist. When he didn't get an answer, he snapped another punch into the same spot. The second punch wasn't as strong as the first, but since he'd already busted the intruder's nose, Slocum knew it hurt a hell of a lot more. "Answer me!"

"I wad jus . . . commin' to ask for somb wahder," the intruder said through his broken nose and the mask of blood that now coated his face.

"You ask for water by sneaking up with a knife in your hand? Try again."

The intruder might have been mumbling something, but his words were washed out by the damage to his nose and the pained breaths he was sucking in through his mouth.

"Who else is with you?" Slocum asked. He raised his fist and held it over the intruder's face long enough for the younger man to get a good look and think about what would happen when that fist came crashing down again. Unfortunately, it was also long enough for the younger man to gather up enough strength to pull his other arm free from Slocum's grasp.

Either the intruder was a bit stronger than Slocum had guessed, or his blood was just running quickly enough to give him the needed jolt to get the job done. Either way, he twisted and pulled until he was once again free to swing the hunting knife.

Slocum cursed under his breath as he fought to regain control of the intruder's weapon. But the more he struggled to get a grip on the younger man's arm, the less Slocum was able to control the rest of him. As the intruder flailed, he managed to squirm out from under Slocum's knee. He didn't even realize what he'd done until Slocum slipped awkwardly to one side and shifted his weight to keep from falling over.

As Slocum's knee pounded against the ground, he let go of the intruder's shirt so he could divert all of his attention to controlling the man's knife hand. Slocum managed to get a loose grip on that arm, but only at the cost of allowing the wiry man to kick his own legs out and away before pulling them up underneath him. Just as the intruder started to straighten up and gain the high ground in the fight, Slocum let go with both hands and brought his own leg around in a powerful sweeping motion.

The intruder had just regained his balance when Slocum kicked his legs out from under him. The sweep caught the intruder just above the ankles and nearly flipped the slender man over sideways before he came crashing down. He hit the dirt on his ribs, but still had plenty of fight left in him.

Slocum was on his feet, looking down at the intruder. His first instinct was to skin the Colt Navy, but he saw the glint of the man's blade flashing through the air before he could clear leather. Hopping back a step, Slocum got the six-shooter from its holster and squeezed off a quick shot. Even though the man was right in front of him, Slocum knew his first shot was a miss. It had been too rushed and he was moving around too much for it to do anything more than kick up a mound of dirt.

That gunshot was still echoing through the night when Slocum pulled his trigger again. Somehow, the intruder was desperate and slippery enough to flip himself onto his belly and scurry straight toward him. Slocum adjusted his aim and prepared to fire again. No man could dance around all six of the Colt's rounds. Before Slocum could prove his theory, the intruder lunged forward and took a swipe at him that had the speed of a snare that had just been tripped.

It was all Slocum could do to keep from being gutted as he hopped away from the blade. After landing on one heel and quickly regaining his balance, Slocum touched his hand to his chest and belly to see if he'd been cut open. He could feel the front of his shirt had a clean rip across the middle, but there was no blood on his fingertips.

Perhaps Slocum needed to put more stock in luck after all.

The intruder came at Slocum wearing a feral snarl upon his face and keeping his body hunkered down low. He gripped the knife so it trailed behind him as he approached. Once he got close enough, however, he snapped his shoulders around to move his arm like a whip.

Tired of backing down, Slocum held his ground and swung his six-gun down to block the intruder's hand. The side of the Colt impacted with the man's forearm, but didn't do much to slow either one down. The intruder was more than happy to remain where he was. In fact, he didn't even seem to feel the pain from his busted nose any longer.

"I'm gonna cut you open," the attacker grunted as he took a quick slash at Slocum, "and then I'm gonna stick somethin' into that lady of yours."

Knowing he didn't have many shots left, Slocum wasn't about to do the intruder a favor by wasting another one. He set his sights on his target and brought up his pistol to fire off another round. A split second before he could squeeze his trigger, Slocum saw the intruder snap his knife out toward his gun hand.

Even if he didn't get a serious cut, that blade could do enough damage to affect Slocum's draw for years to come. If that happened, Slocum's life span could be cut very short indeed. But Slocum's speed was just fine. He pulled that arm back, leaving nothing but the Colt Navy itself to catch a glancing scrape from the intruder's blade. Sparks flew as steel scraped against iron. The intruder twisted his hand to allow the blade to roll along the gun's barrel and then snap upward toward the hand that held it.

Slocum brought his other fist up and around to catch the inside of the intruder's right arm in a short, chopping swing. It wasn't a hit that did any damage, but it diverted the knife before it could draw any more blood. One more push from Slocum was all it took to push that knife out even further, forcing the intruder's arm out and away from his body, leaving his chest completely exposed.

Slocum brought up his leg and threw it out in front of him as if he was kicking in a door. The bottom of his boot made solid contact, taking the intruder completely off his feet. Having seen examples of the man's speed, Slocum didn't waste any time in following up. After the intruder landed flat on his back, Slocum brought his other leg forward to swing at the best target within his range.

As if sensing the foot that was aimed at his nether regions, the intruder rolled onto his side and curled up in an attempt to take the kick in a more protected spot. He was already flipping the knife around in his hand in preparation for his answering swing when Slocum's boot caught him right in the soft spot on the side of his knee.

"Owwwsonofabitch!" the intruder howled as his knee cracked and the bones in his leg ground together.

Even though it hadn't been the kick he was hoping for, Slocum played the cards he'd been dealt. The intruder flopped onto his back again, but reflexively swung at Slocum as he closed in on him. This swing didn't have nearly as much steam as the ones that had preceded it, so Slocum was able to deliver another kick before the blade could find its mark.

Slocum's boot slammed against the intruder's arm, sending the knife into the nearby grass. Before the intruder could make a move to collect his weapon, he found himself staring down the business end of a smoke wagon.

"Eliza!" Slocum shouted as he stared along the top of his Colt and into the bloody face of the intruder. "You all right?"

After a few seconds, Eliza stuck her head up and shakily replied, "Fine. What about you?"

"Just stay put." Lowering his voice and glaring down at the intruder, Slocum asked, "Where are the others?"

"They're all right behind me so—"

Shaking his head as he thumbed back the Colt's hammer, Slocum said, "You can keep that shit to yourself. If there was any more of you assholes skulking around here, they would have been here to back you up or do something to Eliza by now."

The intruder's eyes reflected his fear, and his face started to twitch in at least half a dozen spots. "There's more of them at a camp not too far from here." Upon seeing the shift in Slocum's expression, the intruder quickly amended himself by saying, "They're a few miles out. I scouted ahead to find you. I saw you and that lady were . . . keeping each other busy, so I came in for a closer look."

"Theil sent you?"

Reluctantly, the intruder nodded. "I can tell you how many there are. I can tell you where to find them."

"I don't want to find them."

"Then I can tell you what you're up against."

"I think Eliza already has a good idea of what she's up against. Seeing as how this isn't the first time you boys have made a run at us, I'm getting a good idea as well."

"Then what do you want from me?" the intruder asked.

"What's your name?"

The question obviously caught the man off his guard. He blinked a few times, but couldn't take his eyes away from the gun filling Slocum's hand. "Andy."

"Tell you what, Andy. I want you to let Theil know that me and Eliza don't like it when killers like yourself sneak up to stick a knife in our backs."

Andy nodded vigorously.

Slocum nodded also. Backing up a few steps, he lowered his gun and then finally eased it back into its holster. He relaxed his posture, allowed his shoulders to come down a little, and then began making his way back to camp.

The sound of rustling once more drifted through the air. Unlike the last time he'd heard it, Slocum knew exactly what was causing that sound. He turned to find Andy scrambling for his knife. To the younger man's credit, Andy was fast enough to get to the weapon and cock his arm back to throw it into a spot between Slocum's ribs.

Slocum, on the other hand, was just a bit faster.

The Colt Navy cleared leather with a sound that could barely be heard. Slocum's eyes were already locked onto Andy's face, which was exactly where he intended on putting his next bullet. The pistol bucked once against Slocum's palm and delivered its smoky cargo all the way through Andy's head.

The younger man's brains looked like a dark, greasy mist as they exploded from the back of his skull. Andy's head snapped back as if he'd been kicked, and his back hit the ground with a solid thump. His arms twitched until the last bit of life bled out of him.

As Slocum stepped forward, he pulled his trigger to

empty the pistol into the pulpy remains of Andy's face. There wasn't any need to check on Andy after that. It would have taken a whole lot more than luck for any man to live without a head on his shoulders.

Slocum collected Andy's knife and walked back to the camp.

"Thank God you're all right," Eliza said as she rushed forward to hug Slocum.

After patting her back, Slocum pulled himself out of her grasp and reloaded his Colt. "Gather our things. We're making camp somewhere else."

"What about the man out there?"

"No need to worry about him. He's delivering my message to Theil and the rest of those hired guns."

10

Slocum's message was received early the next morning.

The camp Dawes had set up was small and cold throughout most of the night, since he refused to light any sort of fire. The men huddled in a circle around a spot where a fire should be, gazing down at the empty patch of ground while wrapped up in their blankets. They'd begun speaking to one another once they thawed out a bit after the sun came up. When a lone man on horseback approached the camp, the men had something to talk about.

"Where's Andy?" Dawes asked. "You find him?"

"Yeah, I found him," Lem replied. "He's dead. Least I'm pretty sure it's him."

All the men stood up and fixed their eyes intently upon Lem.

Tossing out the rest of his water, Dawes asked, "What do you mean you're pretty sure?"

"Ain't much of a face left. Hell, there ain't much of a head."

"Jesus. You gotta know whether or not it was him, dammit! Even if you recognize some of his clothes."

Lem swung down from his saddle and rubbed his hands together to warm them up. "I didn't dress the son of a bitch.

He looked like any one of us if we got our damn heads blown off. Some animals got to him overnight, so—"

"Get back on that horse," Dawes snapped. "Take me to the spot where you found him."

Letting out an aggravated sigh, Lem looked over at the rest of the men. There were only two more apart from Dawes, and not even the hint of a fire. There wasn't any food being passed around, so Lem climbed into his saddle without much more complaint.

"What about that bitch and her hired gun?" Dawes asked. "I don't suppose you found them?"

"Yeah. I got 'em both wrapped up for a surprise and wasn't gonna say a word about it."

Dawes grumbled to himself and fetched his horse from where they were all tethered. Mark and the remaining man shrugged and sat back down. After Lem and Dawes rode away, they scrambled to put together a fire and have a proper breakfast.

By the time Lem and Dawes arrived at the spot where Slocum and Eliza had made their first camp, the sun was bright in the sky and the wind blew in fiercely from the west. Lem rode straight to the spot where a crumpled body lay sprawled out and covered in filth. Dawes took his time in getting there. He looked around at every detail. All the while, he kept his hand upon the gun holstered at his side.

"Right here," Lem said as he dismounted. "Have a look for yourself."

Dawes looked at the dead body and let out a disgusted breath. The coppery scent of blood was thick in the air, and was mixed with the sour stench of meat that was starting to turn. Lem was right in his assessment that animals had been picking at the body. The edges of Andy's clothes were tattered and pulled away to expose bits of flesh that had been gnawed on and chewed.

"Looks like Andy to me," Dawes said. "Whoever did this wanted to leave a hell of a mess for us to find."

"You think he left anything else behind?"

"I don't know. Why don't you take a closer look?"

"Shit," Lem mumbled. "I had ta ask."

After steeling himself, Lem approached the body and winced as he got close enough for more of the smells to hit him. "Awww, for Christ's sake. Somethin' gutted him."

"Gut-shot?"

"No. Looks like he was ripped open by some damned thing."

"Just check for anything that can tell us for certain if that's Andy and stop telling me about every animal bite. I'll go look at the camp."

Dawes rode over the branches spread around the dirt that had been kicked over the small campfire. After dismounting, he walked the perimeter of the camp and then circled around again. He didn't expect to find anything.

"It's him all right!" Lem shouted from where he was kneeling. "The knife's gone, but he's still got that fancy scabbard on his belt."

"He got pretty damn close to where they were camping," Dawes said.

"If it was even them two."

"It was. Andy was a hell of a scout and he wouldn't have bothered closing in on a camp if it wasn't the one he was after. He probably took a wrong step and snapped one of them branches that are strewn about. After that . . . well . . . seems clear enough what happened after that."

Lem walked over to the camp and pulled in a few breaths now that he was upwind of the body. "There was a fight. Plenty of scuffle marks and blood spilled."

Dawes had moved away from the middle of the abandoned camp and was crouching down to get a closer look at the ground. "Here's some tracks."

Rushing over to Dawes, Lem looked down and nodded enthusiastically. "Sure as hell! Them tracks can't be more'n a couple hours old!"

Furrowing his brow as he studied the tracks, Dawes held

back from speaking his mind. There wasn't any way to be certain just how old the tracks were, but they were fresher than most of the markings left on the ground and they led away from a spot where at least two horses had obviously been kept. Without anything else to contribute, there wasn't any reason to bicker about the details.

"Come on," Dawes ordered. "Let's see where these tracks lead to."

"Should I get Mark and that other one?"

"His name's Edmonson. And will you at least take a good look at him? If you'd been paying attention better, we wouldn't have had to waste all the time gawking at that damned corpse."

Lem muttered under his breath and collected his horse. After Dawes snapped his reins and rode off to follow those tracks, Lem watched to take note of where the big man was headed. He then pointed his horse's nose in the direction from which they'd come and tapped his heels against the animal's sides.

Dawes almost rode straight past the second camp. With the sunlight still coming in at a low angle, a tall boulder cast a long shadow over what looked like just another bump along the side of the road. The tracks disappeared a bit farther along, which brought Dawes back around to that boulder and bump.

There weren't any tracks leading directly to that spot, but Dawes only had to take a moment to think about where he'd make camp after his first one was found by a sneaky cuss like Andy. Dawes climbed down from his horse's back and walked over to the small pile of dirt. A few kicks revealed a pile of wood that was still slightly warm to the touch. Not too far from that spot, there was a cigarette butt lying half buried in the dirt. Dawes reached out to take the remains of the cigarette and touched his finger to the burnt end. It wasn't warm, but it told him what he'd wanted to know.

"You two were here, all right," he said to himself. "And I suppose there aren't many different ways for you to go from here."

Dawes turned toward the west and squinted at the open country spread out before him. The rugged terrain rose and fell like an ocean of rock that had been frozen in the middle of a squall. Trees poked up here and there, but weren't clustered together enough to provide any real cover. After retrieving the field glasses from his saddlebag, Dawes surveyed the land one more time.

Even though he hadn't been expecting to spot the riders he was after, Dawes still cursed under his breath when he came up empty. He then turned completely around to study the path he'd taken to get to the camp. This time, Dawes spotted something. Lem and the other two men must have been moving like wildfire because they were close enough for Dawes to see them through the field glasses.

Unable to stand and wait for them to arrive, Dawes mounted up and raced back to meet up with them. He only needed to get close enough for the men to spot him before Dawes motioned and turned his horse back around. The three men followed in Dawes's tracks, and caught up with him before they got too far past the second camp. Once the group was reunited, the combined sound of their horses was like thunder rolling over the barren New Mexico landscape. Dawes didn't care about that. He knew the two they were chasing were moving too quickly to hear what was coming up behind them.

If Eliza Banner or that hired gun of hers did know Dawes was coming, they would either turn and fight, keep running, or find someplace to hide. Each choice was fine with Dawes. He outnumbered them two to one. Getting ahead of them would only make things difficult for Banner. If they kept running, Dawes would catch up to them sooner rather than later.

Grinning at his prospects, Dawes pulled his bandanna up

over his mouth and nose to keep from swallowing too much dust.

Finding the second camp had been helpful. Picking up a fresh set of tracks was even better. Before he got too worked up, however, Dawes kept his men moving and rarely took the field glasses away from his eyes. Making matters a little easier for him was the fact that water was becoming awfully scarce along this stretch of trail.

The last stream they'd found was little more than a trickle of dirty rainwater running over a flat bed of rocks. Dawes had raced right past that water to try and gain some more ground on Banner. The tracks they'd found led them to a watering hole that was marked by the skeletal remains of an old shed. With his own horse starting to wheeze under the strain of constantly running, Dawes motioned for the others to slow down.

"Let's catch our breath and water the horses," Dawes said. "But don't get comfortable. We're movin' on again soon."

The others were so happy to hear the first part that they barely seemed to notice the second. The entire group brought their horses to a stop alongside the watering hole, and the men dismounted to stretch their legs. Canteens were filled and not much was said as the horses lapped up the standing water.

Dawes surveyed the land through the field glasses and came up empty once again. He walked over to the shack to have a look inside on the off chance that someone else might have used the rickety structure for a resting spot. The only thing within those four broken walls was more dirt and what looked to be a few old animals' nests. By the smell of the place, it was still being used as a home for some kind of critter or another.

"Find anything?"

Those two words nearly caused Dawes to jump out of his skin. Turning toward Mark, Dawes replied, "Nothing but some animal scat. What about you?"

"Lem's looking around the watering hole right now."

"What about that other fella?"

"You mean Edmonson? He's not even looking. Andy was the scout. It's a damn shame what happened to him. A damn surprise, too. He was supposed to be real good."

"It looked like he just got anxious. I told you someone else should have gone along with him."

Dropping his voice a bit, Mark said, "That's what Edmonson's been griping about all this time. He says if he was there, that gunman Banner hired would be dead and—"

"And he'd be the big hero of the day," Dawes snapped. "All the talk in the world don't make things any different. Why didn't he come with us when we caught up with Banner and her hired gun back in East Padre? Where the hell were they then? I'll tell you where. Off getting their knobs polished in a goddamn whorehouse, that's where!"

Even though Dawes didn't seem concerned with lowering his voice, the old shack created just enough of an echo to make his voice travel even farther. Mark looked over to the watering hole to find Edmonson glaring back at him.

"I think he heard you," Mark said.

"Good. Maybe he'll stop his goddamn whining and prove he's worth his pay."

"I'll earn my keep just as soon as you find someone for me to shoot, fat man!" Edmonson hollered from where he was standing. He was a tall fellow who wore a battered duster that was currently tied to both legs to keep it from flapping while he rode. Even with the coat held in place, the double-rig holster around his waist was easy enough to see. Edmonson stood with his hand down close to the gun on his right side.

Dawes shoved Mark out of his way as he stomped over to the man in the duster. "You feeling brave? You itching for a fight? What the hell are you waiting for then?"

Edmonson took a few steps forward, and would have met Dawes halfway if Mark hadn't run around to put himself between them. Mark held out both arms as if he fully intended to shove the two men back.

"We got enough to do without this bullshit!" Mark said.

Without so much as glancing at Mark, Edmonson slipped his hand beneath his coat to reach for one of his holstered pistols. Dawes reached for his own gun, but was at least a full second behind the other man. Because Edmonson's hand snagged upon his duster, he and Dawes both cleared leather at the same time. Before any shots were fired, Lem shouted from back at the watering hole.

"I got 'em!"

Without taking his eyes off Edmonson, Dawes asked, "Got who?"

"That bitch and her gunfighter! It's got to be them."

Dawes furrowed his brow to glare at Edmonson. Both men scowled at each other, but lowered their guns back into their holsters. After Dawes had gone over to check on Lem, Mark stayed behind to keep an eye on Edmonson.

"That fat prick better watch his mouth," Edmonson said.

"You might wanna do the same," Mark warned. "Me and Lem have been riding with Dawes longer than we've known you. Besides, it ain't as if Mr. Theil is gonna pay us more if the rest of us get killed. We only get paid for doin' our job and we won't get squat unless that job gets done."

Whether those words sunk in or not, Edmonson straightened his duster so it covered his holster again and walked over to where his horse was still lapping up water.

Mark went to Dawes and Lem, making an effort to keep Edmonson where he could see him.

Dawes was hunkering down at a spot on the opposite side of the watering hole from where their own horses were drinking. "You get him straightened out?" he asked.

"His partner's dead," Mark replied. "He's probably just riled up about that. What'd you find, Lem?"

Lem was hunched over and fidgeting with his broken spectacles. Even though he had to keep shifting them upon his nose and squinting through them at different angles, he still seemed happy about what he saw. "I found some tracks. They're fresh enough that they gotta be them."

"It's them all right," Dawes said.

When he looked over at the big man, Mark saw that Dawes wasn't even looking at the tracks Lem had found. "How do you know?" he asked.

Dawes held something in one hand, which he kept waving under his nose. Grinning after pulling in a few sniffs, he extended his hand to show the cigarette butt that he'd pulled from the dirt. "I picked this up a few paces from this spot. It's the same tobacco that was in a cigarette I found at the other camp Lem and I found."

"You sure it's the same?"

Dawes nodded. "Smells expensive and not like anything any old cowboy would smoke. Besides, I just smelled the other stuff this morning, so I recall the scent. You say you found tracks leading from here?"

"Yep," Lem replied. "And they're headed west."

"Perfect."

Now that they had a definite task to perform, all the men were more interested in carrying that out than bickering with one another. Despite this sense of purpose, neither Dawes nor Edmonson was about to let the other ride behind him. Those two remained at the back of the group, with Lem leading the way and Mark keeping his eye on either side of the trail.

Dawes occasionally looked through his field glasses, but lowered them at irregular intervals to sneak a quick glance over to see what Edmonson was doing.

More often than not, Edmonson was watching the other three like a hawk. Every now and then, he took a look around to see if he might actually spot the folks he'd been hired to find.

Amazingly enough, the group made fairly good progress. The land opened up around them, which made it easier to spot movement in nearly every direction. Things got a little difficult when the sound of the horses' hooves rumbling against packed soil shifted to a clatter as the dirt beneath them gave way to rock.

"You still see them tracks, Lem?" Dawes shouted.

"Just hold yer water," Lem grumbled as he pulled back on his reins so he could climb down from his saddle.

"What the hell are we stopping for?" Edmonson asked. His hand had already drifted to the gun on his right hip.

Lem was hunkered down and squinting at the rocks that jutted from the ground and the stone that was exposed as the thin layer of dirt was blown away. "Just give me a second, will ya? All that shouting ain't helping a damn thing!"

Edmonson kept quiet, but he shifted to keep all of the other men in his sights. The jerky movement made it look as if he'd suddenly become very uncomfortable in his saddle.

Lem had to backtrack a little ways, but he finally straightened up and jabbed a finger at the ground. "There you are, you son of a bitch! I got ya!"

"What?" Mark asked.

"A shoed horse came along this way. There's scrape marks on the ground. Come see for yerself if you don't believe me."

"Was it the same horses that left those other tracks?" Dawes asked.

"Ain't no way to know," Lem replied. "I can tell ya these scrapes are fresh. They're still colored by—"

"Fine," Dawes interrupted. "Can you follow them?"

"They're not as regular as normal tracks, since not every step is gonna leave a scrape and some parts of the rock might not hold the markings—"

"Can you follow them?"

Looking up at Dawes, Lem shrugged and then nodded. "We won't be able to ride as fast, but yeah. I can follow them."

Already peering through his field glasses, Dawes said, "It looks like this rock shifts back to dirt before too long. Keep us going in the right direction and we'll pick up the trail once we get some softer ground beneath us."

"Why don't we just ride ahead to Bray?" Edmonson asked. "Ain't that where they're headed?"

"If Mr. Theil wanted to meet up with her in Bray, he

wouldn't have sent us to East Padre in the first place, ass-hole!" Mark growled.

Dawes aimed at Mark's head and thumbed his hammer back. "I'm sick of your fucking mouth," he snarled. "You want to take charge so bad? You should've proven yourself to be something more than a useless stack of horseshit piled beneath a hat when Mr. Theil was doing the hiring! You want to step up now? Go on and make your move."

Mark didn't move. He glared plenty hard at Dawes, but didn't move.

Nodding slowly, Dawes lowered his gun.

"All's I meant," Mark grumbled, "was that we won't get the bonus if . . ." Suddenly, Mark stopped talking.

After a few seconds, Edmonson asked, "Bonus? What bonus?"

"The bonus Mr. Theil offered if we keep that cheating bitch from setting foot in Bray," Dawes explained. "Of course, if we can catch up to her and put her down, you'll get a cut of the bonus as well."

Edmonson nodded. "Of course I will. Much obliged."

"Yeah," Lem snarled as he locked a murderous glare onto Mark. "Much obliged."

11

Slocum and Eliza rode hard for the entire latter half of the day. They would have ridden just as hard throughout the first portion of the day, but Slocum had made better use of those hours.

It had all started simply enough. He'd awakened before sunrise, rolled a cigarette, started a small fire, and cooked up just enough coffee to fill two cups. The fire was barely large enough to get the job done, but that also meant it wasn't large enough to create a big flame or send up too much smoke. When he was finished, he nudged Eliza with his toe and set the dented tin cup down next to her.

She stirred a bit, but didn't wake up. In fact, Slocum had to nudge her twice more before she even rolled over onto her side.

"Come on," Slocum said. "Rise and shine."

One of her eyes came open and immediately closed. "The sun isn't even rised and shined."

"Rised isn't a word. Just get up and drink your coffee."

"Coffee? What about breakfast?"

Since Slocum obviously wasn't going anywhere, she dragged herself up and almost knocked over the coffee in the process. "You can make coffee, but you can't make breakfast? Where's the fire?"

"It's out already."

"Damn it, I would have liked some bacon. Would that have been so hard?"

Slocum chuckled and shook his head. "You're a real peach, you know that? When's the last time you slept with ground under you instead of a goose-down pillow?"

"It's been a while. The last time I slept outside, it was—"

"Sorry. I didn't expect an answer to that. Just drink your coffee and get yourself ready. We're in a rush."

Eliza sipped her coffee and gathered her things, making certain to complain every inch of the way. To her credit, she managed to finish up in less time than Slocum had figured it would take her. Of course, since they'd packed up and ridden to the second camp in a hurry after Andy had found the first one the night before, Slocum hadn't allowed her to take much of anything out of the saddlebags.

"All ready to go?" Slocum asked.

"Yes."

"Good. Now you can pick out whatever you absolutely have to keep so we can both ride on one horse."

"What?" Eliza gasped. "But my horse is just fine! There's plenty of room in my bags."

"I know. That way, there'll be plenty of room for some of the things I don't need. And if that doesn't fill those bags up," Slocum added as he let out a smoky breath, "we'll pack some rocks in."

Eliza's brow furrowed into an angry glare. Then her expression shifted into something else entirely. "If you want me to ride with you, all you need to do is ask."

"You will be riding with me."

"That's fine. And we can just let my horse trail along."

Slocum nodded and snuffed his cigarette out into a small mound of nearby dirt. "That's the plan. Your horse will trail along until we hit a suitable spot to let it go. After that, we'll—"

"That's *my* horse," Eliza said as the anger returned to her face. "I'm the one paying you for this job, Mr. Slocum. I won't allow this sort of nonsense if it means me having to rid myself of a perfectly good horse. Not without some sort of explanation!"

"You'll get your explanation," Slocum assured her. "After we pack everything up and get moving. They could be arriving here any minute."

Slocum figured that last part would cut right to the quick. Sure enough, Eliza pulled her eyes away from him and looked in every other direction. "They could be here anytime?" she asked skittishly. "You mean Theil's men?"

"I sure don't mean a group of wandering missionaries. You want to get moving or would you rather wait here and fight it out?" Taking a glance around for himself, Slocum nodded slowly and said, "Come to think of it, this might not be a bad spot to make a stand. You get a rifle and point it that way. I'll cover that direction and we can pick one or two of them off when they make a run at us. We'll probably catch some lead ourselves, but at least one of us should make it through in one piece as long as they don't try to pick us off from a distance. You think they'd try something like that?"

Eliza didn't look too angry and she didn't even look too frightened. Instead, there was a healthy mix of both on her face, along with a good dose of good old-fashioned annoyance. "You made your point, John. Let's get moving, but I want my explanation."

"You'll get it."

"I'm not parting with my horse until I do!"

Rather than spur her on with any more words, Slocum raised his hands in surrender and hurried with the last of his preparations.

They rode away from the camp before the sun had fully risen. The morning was chilly, but there was warmth building in the air, so the lingering cold washed over them like a splash of cool water on a hot day. A few deep breaths filled Slocum's lungs with earthy scents and swelled his chest like a set of full sails.

"So you think Theil's men will track us down?" Eliza asked.

"I'm counting on it," Slocum replied.

"What happens when they do? You suppose they're following us right now?"

"That man they sent out last night was a scout. He was there to get in close and do some damage if he could. I believe that much of what he told me, since he wouldn't have been alone if he was just another killer. Besides, I kept watch most of the night and nobody came near us."

"But you said you were counting on them tracking us down."

Slocum nodded and snapped his reins to build up some more speed. His horse quickened its pace until the reins looped around its saddle horn drew taut. Eliza's horse responded fast enough and trotted alongside. After a few more push-and-pull exchanges like that, both animals found their rhythm.

"They're out here to track us down," Slocum said. "The only way to stop that would be to kill them all or pay them to turn tail and run. I'm not of a mind to do either, so we're throwing them off the trail."

Eliza tightened her arms around Slocum's midsection and asked, "How do you intend on doing that?"

"I started by breaking into some expensive tobacco I was saving for the right occasion."

"Tobacco?"

"Yep. Real fine stuff. Has a real distinct smell that's just the right side of sweet. I smoked a cigarette just before we broke that first camp, then I smoked another this morning, and I intend on having another when we stop to water the horses. That way, when Theil's men find the second camp, they've got something to connect the two and go where we lead them."

"You think they'll pick up on the cigarettes like that?" Eliza asked.

"Any tracker worth his salt would. If they don't, then we shouldn't be in any real danger of being caught anyhow. It's always safer to assume the worst, though."

"It's like that in poker, too." Suddenly, Eliza said, "Is that why you made a fire this morning, but didn't want to cook much of anything?"

Nodding, Slocum told her, "I left just enough to mark that spot as a camp. Even a half-blind tracker should be able to pick up on that much. From there, they'll follow the tracks we're laying down right now."

"And then what?"

"Then we wait to find a good spot to part company with your horse. I was thinking of a nice shallow stream or river where we could ride in some water, but I believe there's a stretch of dry rock ahead that will do just as well."

Eliza leaned to one side so she could look around Slocum. They were riding at a good pace and plenty of wind whipped into her face. Squinting at the trail ahead while holding her hat on with one hand, she was finally able to get a look at the spot Slocum was pointing at. She didn't see what he was talking about until Slocum handed back his field glasses. It was a section of ground where the trail widened out and loose dirt gave way to a bare, rocky floor. As far as she could tell, the rock was actually a section of a hill that sloped gently upward to the west. It wasn't a treacherous bit of trail, but anyone with eyes in their head could tell it would be trickier to see tracks once there was rock as opposed to soil under a horse's hooves.

"We'll lead them to that stretch of rock," Slocum explained. "They'll pick up what they can, but it'll only be what we leave for them. When they pick up our trail beyond that rock bed, it'll lead them to wherever your horse decides to go."

"Wherever my horse decides to go?"

Even though Slocum could tell by the tone in her voice that Eliza was putting the pieces together on her own, he could also tell that she needed him to spell it out anyway. "We're setting your horse loose to go on its way. We'll ride my horse, circle around a few miles up, and then make our way to Bray. It may take us a bit longer, but Theil's men will be slowed up as well and they won't cross our path."

Eliza let out a frustrated sigh. "Why don't we just face them? You've handled those gunmen before. Why not just do it again?"

"Because they'll be ready for it. My guess is they're more than willing to flush us out and then have a rifleman hang back to pick us off from a distance. I never saw that scout until last night, so there's no telling how many more men are in that group. Even if we don't know how many there are, it's safe to figure they outnumber us. All of that means that facing them down on their terms in this sort of open country isn't the best idea."

"And here I thought you were just going to tell me to keep quiet," Eliza grumbled.

"Would you have kept quiet?" Slocum didn't get an answer, but he could feel Eliza shifting her weight behind him. "Didn't think so," he said. "Besides, you are the one paying for my help, so there's no reason I shouldn't tell you what my plan is. If you don't like it, you're within your rights to object. We can part ways now, and I'm sure you can figure the odds on you making it all the way to your cherished card game before those gunmen get ahold of you."

Now Slocum felt Eliza's head bump against his shoulder. She bumped him again as if she was butting her head against the proverbial brick wall. "I really liked that horse," she whined.

They kept riding toward the dry rock bed, and Slocum brought both horses to a stop once they reached it. After loading up Eliza's horse with enough weight to get close to equaling the weight of a rider, he led it onto the rock bed and steered it in a southerly direction. Slocum hated to let a good horse go and Eliza's horse was definitely no slouch, but he knew the horse wasn't going to waste. In fact, if it did what Slocum hoped, that horse might just be the key to them getting to Bray.

The horse was reluctant to leave at first, but Slocum looped the reins around its saddle horn so they drooped down to brush against its side. He then took his hat off, swatted its rump a bit harder, and let out a sharp *yah* to get it going. Those things did the trick and the horse took off at a healthy gallop. It knew well enough its saddle was empty, but the shock of Slocum's swats and the brush of the reins against its side kept the horse moving long enough for its natural instincts to take over. Once it set its mind to running, it was off like a shot.

"All right," Slocum said. "You're going to point yourself to the northeast and ride ahead of me."

"How far?"

Turning around to get a look behind him, Slocum squinted and then took his field glasses from out of his saddlebag. After studying the view for a few seconds, he said, "It doesn't look like they're nipping at our heels just yet, but I've got to figure they've at least found the second camp by now."

"They're not all that bright, remember?"

"Well, if not by now, they should be stumbling on the camp soon. After that, it won't take long before they're close enough to catch sight of us." Slocum kept the field glasses in his hand and walked along the stretch of rock that Eliza's horse had raced over. Sure enough, there were scrapes along the rock here and there to mark the spots where the horse's shoes had hit. "Hold up, Eliza."

She pulled back on her reins, and watched as Slocum pulled the bandanna from around his neck. He examined the material and then ripped it in half.

"Give me your bandanna," he said.

"If you want me to undress, that's the long road to take," she replied.

Slocum tried to keep his mind on the task at hand, which meant ignoring that remark altogether. Once he had her bandanna, he ripped it in half. From there, Slocum dropped to one knee so he could get to his horse's front left hoof. The horse fidgeted a bit, and even started to shake its leg in protest until it got a look at who was causing its grief. The horse was reluctant and a bit uneasy, but it let Slocum wrap its hoof with half of a bandanna.

None of the hooves were easier to wrap than any other. In

fact, the horse became more agitated as Slocum made his rounds. When he was done, Slocum looked down and grinned at his handiwork. "It's not perfect, but it'll do."

"Will that be enough to keep it from leaving marks?" Eliza asked.

"Not completely, but it should be enough to keep the marks from being too noticeable. At the very least, they'll be less noticeable than the ones your horse is putting down right about now. Either way, it's going to have to be enough. We've dawdled too long already."

"Yes, sir," Eliza said as she gave the reins a flick.

The horse took its first few steps as if it had suddenly found itself upon a frozen pond. A few steps after that, it fidgeted some more and started to lean down to nip at the wrappings covering its shoes. To her credit, Eliza didn't panic when the horse began to fret. She kept her balance and tugged on the reins just enough to discourage it from fussing too long with either of its front hooves.

"You might want to do the riding, John," she said warily.

"You're doing fine," Slocum told her as he reached out to pat the horse's neck and walked alongside.

The horse snapped its head around as if it meant to bite off a few of Slocum's fingers. When it got a look at the stern glint in Slocum's eyes, the horse let out a few annoyed huffs and pointed its nose forward again.

Still focusing on the look in his eyes and the warning tilt of his head, Slocum kept his hand on the horse's neck and gave it a few encouraging pats once it refrained from biting him. Now that the lines had been drawn and the pecking order was in place, Slocum felt comfortable that the horse would put one foot in front of the other just like it was supposed to. Of course, judging by the way it hung its head and huffed every couple of breaths, the horse wasn't at all happy about it.

The sounds of Eliza's horse clomping away drifted through the air. Once those sounds had faded, Slocum couldn't hear much of anything else other than the wind and the muted thump of his own horse's steps. Once the horse got a little more comfortable in its footing, Slocum gave Eliza the order to speed up.

She flicked her reins and the horse responded by lurching forward into an awkward run.

Slocum followed on foot and did his best to clean up the few scrapes his horse left behind. There wasn't a lot for him to do in that regard, but he brushed away the marks with a bunch of twigs he'd collected and kept working to keep his horse's trail from being spotted. After that, he touched up the scrapes left behind by Eliza's horse to make certain they weren't missed.

If those hired guns couldn't pick up the trail Slocum gave them, they weren't any kind of threat in the first place.

If Theil's men saw through Slocum's effort to throw them off, they would wish they'd never started their hunt.

12

The dry rock bed only went on for another two miles before Eliza reached its eastern edge. Once there was dirt beneath her and more dirt on the trail ahead, she pulled back on her reins and fought to get Slocum's horse to stand still. Now that the horse had been snapped out of its rhythm, it scraped at the ground and fussed even more.

The plan was for her to continue in a straight line until she got someplace where she could wait for Slocum to catch up to them. Before the horse could work itself up into a lather, she snapped the reins and steered it more or less in the right direction.

Unfortunately, there wasn't much of a choice as far as hiding places were concerned. The best she could find was a tree that was tall enough to cast her and the horse in some shade. Riding out any farther than that would have only forced Slocum to walk more. Eliza reached the tree in no time and wrestled the horse to a stop. Even though the horse was no longer going forward, it kept its legs moving as it stomped and whinnied with renewed vigor.

"Oh, no, you don't," Eliza snapped as she continued to wrestle the animal. "Hold still, damn it. You'll just leave deeper tracks to be found."

As soon as the horse stood still long enough, Eliza hopped from the saddle and took a few steps back. She eyed the horse carefully, but didn't think the big fellow was going to start bucking. After steeling herself with a nice, deep breath, she stretched out both arms and approached the horse the way she'd seen Slocum do it the last few times.

"Easy now," she said soothingly. "I can help you if you keep still."

The horse shook its head and swung it toward the sound of her voice. Eliza's first reaction was to duck and back away at the same time. Doing both things too quickly, however, caused her to lose her balance. She stumbled for half a step, saw the horse turn and swing its back legs around toward her and then plant its two front ones.

"Oh, sh—" was all Eliza could spit out before the horse leaned forward and snapped one of its rear legs in her direction like a dog trying to dry off one of its paws. Unlike a dog's, this leg had enough force to break Eliza's arm or even snap her neck if it caught her right.

She tried to back up some more, but only lost the last bit of balance that was keeping her upright. Eliza fell onto her back just as one of the horse's rear legs snapped over her. Rolling to one side, Eliza scrambled away from the horse, and then realigned herself to get a look at the pissed-off animal.

Just as she was about to approach the horse again, Eliza noticed the big fellow had turned to look at her directly. Although Eliza might have spent more time in saloons and poker halls than in corrals or stables, she could feel the thin line she was currently treading. On one side of that line, the horse would settle down and let her get closer. On the other side, it would lash out and possibly knock her head off with one well-placed kick.

The only thing that spurred Eliza to keep walking that line was the fact that the horse continued to scrape and pound at the dirt so long as those bandannas were wrapped around its hooves. She simply couldn't take the chance on leaving such a prominent set of markings upon the ground when they'd spent the better part of the day treading so carefully.

"All right," she said in her soothing tone. "I'm getting those things off your feet. Won't that be nice?"

When Eliza took a few careful half steps forward, the horse arched its neck and glared at her through the wide eye that was pointed in her direction.

Eliza could feel the horse's tension through every one of her muscles. She'd heard of men getting their heads cracked open by wild horses by accident. Approaching an angry horse like this one on purpose seemed to be an even worse idea. It was too late to stop now, though. Moving away could set the animal off just as much as moving toward it, so she figured she might as well try to finish what she'd started.

"Easy now," she cooed. "You're going to feel so much better. Just give me a second and I'll scratch that itch that's been bothering you all this time."

As she spoke, Eliza slowly reached out for the horse's left foreleg. Slocum had tied a large knot to keep the bandanna in place, probably in expectation of needing to pull the bandanna loose without a lot of work. Eliza got to within an inch of the knot, but didn't want to make any sudden moves because the horse was still watching her like a hawk.

She didn't speed up and she didn't slow down. Eliza just kept reaching out at the same speed at which she'd started. As soon as her fingers touched the knot, she could feel the horse start to pull its leg away. Choosing that moment to make her move, Eliza snagged the end of the bandanna between her thumb and forefinger and then pulled it loose.

The horse let out a deep, rumbling breath and shuffled sideways away from her. Every one of its steps annoyed it more and more until it finally started to rock in a series of movements that got dangerously close to bucking.

In her haste to get away from the horse, Eliza stumbled and bumped her rear end on the ground. She quickly pulled her legs in so she could stand up. Once she was upright again, she realized she still held the strip of bandanna in her hand. "There," she sputtered. "See? That wasn't so bad."

The horse wasn't listening to her. Instead, it was working itself into a tizzy and huffing louder and louder as its three wrapped hooves kept thumping against the ground. And then, just when Eliza was wondering how mad Slocum would be when she told him his horse had bolted, the horse put its weight onto the hoof that had been unwrapped.

At first, the horse looked confused.

Then, after a few more steps to test the waters, it realized that one of its hooves wasn't bothering it as much as the others. It took a few more steps before finally settling into a subtle shifting between its three other legs.

"See?" Eliza said breathlessly. "I told you that would be better. How about I fix up those other three?"

The horse's temper had cooled a bit, but it was still watching her carefully as Eliza approached again.

Oddly enough, Eliza felt a little tenser when she went in this time. She hunkered down so her legs were coiled beneath her and she was ready to jump away if the need arose. The horse was keeping still, but that only made Eliza feel as if she was approaching a silent bear trap that was itching to be sprung.

Her first stop was the horse's left hind leg, simply because it was closer than the others. She reached out to grab the end of the bandanna, caught it between her fingers, and pulled. The strip of torn cotton slipped out of her grasp before she could finish pulling, which left the bandanna mostly in place.

The horse shifted its weight, causing Eliza to imagine getting kicked into next week. In the end, the horse wound up adjusting its stance so less weight was placed upon the leg where Eliza was crouching. It then swung its head around to take in its surroundings.

"Oh," Eliza sighed more to herself than to the horse. "That's all? All right. Let's get this over with."

She reached out to pull the bandanna away, and then walked around to the other side of the horse. Having practiced on the other two legs, she didn't have any trouble whatsoever in freeing up those bandannas. In fact, the horse even lifted the appropriate leg to make it easier for her to unwrap each one. When it was over, the horse lowered its head down to sample some clumps of grass sprouting nearby.

Eliza stood with the bandannas in her hands. She glanced back and forth between the dirty shreds of material and the horse's hooves a few times before she allowed herself to let out the breath she'd been holding. The horse turned its head toward her, and then took a step forward. Eliza froze in her tracks, knowing that running away would only make it worse when the horse finally stomped her into the ground.

But the stomping didn't come.

There was only silence for a few seconds before Eliza finally forced herself to open her eyes. The horse was close enough to take up all of her field of vision, but it wasn't the sight she'd been expecting. Rather than vent its anger or throw a tantrum, the horse merely sniffed at the bandannas in her hands and then bumped its nose against Eliza's arm before getting back to its grazing.

Eliza smiled and looked once more at the ripped bandannas she was holding. Suddenly, it seemed awfully silly for those things to have made her fear for life and limb only a few short moments ago. Chuckling to herself, she stuffed the bandannas into her pocket and patted the horse on its neck. "That wasn't so bad."

The horse twitched in her direction, causing Eliza to nearly jump out of her skin.

It was another few hours before Eliza caught sight of anything bigger than a jackrabbit moving beyond the spot where she and the horse were waiting. For a moment, she thought she was just looking at another sort of animal, but once she was able to pick out the shape of a crouching man running in a straight line, she jumped to her feet and waved her arms over her head.

After another few minutes, Slocum was close enough to stop running, drop onto the ground, and catch his breath.

"What took you so long?" Eliza asked. "I was worried sick."

Slocum pulled in a few more breaths and looked at his horse. "What happened to his wrappings? Did they come off somewhere?"

"No. I took them off. He's really pretty nice once he gets to know you. Now where the hell have you been?"

"We part ways for a little bit and you start being friendlier to the horse than to me." Slocum chuckled. "That's nice."

"Oh, stop it. Where were you?"

"In case you forgot, I had to walk for a few miles while you got to ride. Before I got too far, I spotted Theil's men approaching the rock bed."

"Oh, my God," she gasped. "Did they see you?"

"No. There wasn't a lot of places to hide out there, so I had to lay on my belly behind some scrub bushes. I got real familiar with a few big spiders, but I wasn't spotted. Before they could look too hard in my direction, those gunmen found something else to hold their interest."

A hopeful grin showed upon Eliza's face. "Those other tracks?"

"They had to follow one of their men who was on foot and looking for the marks, but they were all led off by your horse."

Eliza beamed proudly and looked to the south as though she could see her horse running like the wind. "And you said you didn't believe in luck."

"Luck?" Slocum grunted. "I break my back all damn day getting those killers to go on a wild-goose chase and you call it luck?"

"I just meant . . ." Rather than finish what she meant to say, Eliza went over to fetch the canteen hanging from Slocum's saddle. Slocum had already sat down with his back against the tree, and was leaning his head back while checking his eyelids for holes. "Here," she said. "You've earned this."

Slocum opened his eyes and took the canteen from her. "I've earned a lot more than this, but it's a start."

She was smiling when Slocum tipped back the canteen, and was still smiling when he lowered it. As tired as he was, it was hard to see that smirk on Eliza's pretty face without grudgingly showing her one of his own. "We'll cross paths with those gunmen once we get to Bray, you know," he said. "You sure this game is worth all that trouble?"

"If I don't go to this game, I'll just have to go through the trouble of untangling whatever lies Theil told about me when he was there, and I'll just have to face them again the next time he finds me. Besides, I already paid my entry fee into the big game."

"Oh, I see. All of this is just so you don't lose an entry fee? That's a kick to the head."

While Eliza appeared somewhat offended by what Slocum said, she couldn't exactly deny it either. "Well," she told him, "two thousand dollars is two thousand dollars."

"Damn," Slocum said with genuine surprise. "I suppose I can't really blame you after all."

Once Slocum had caught his breath and taken a few more swigs of water, he climbed into his saddle and helped Eliza climb up behind him. She wrapped her arms around his midsection and rested her head against his shoulder. At times throughout the day, it seemed as if she was nestling against him and squeezing him tightly. At other times, Eliza simply fell asleep.

Slocum was confident that Theil's men were firmly set upon the wrong trail, but he wasn't about to take stupid chances. He rode in a path that looped around to the north, planning on steering west and then southwest again, which should take Eliza and him to the northern end of Bray. Having spent more time than he'd intended on that rock bed, Slocum knew they would get there later than he'd anticipated. His horse seemed to have other ideas in that regard.

Now that it had the annoying wraps removed from its ankles and plenty of wide-open country in which to run, Slocum's horse seemed more than willing to take full advantage of the situation. When Slocum so much as thought about snapping the reins, his horse took off like he'd been fired from a cannon. Rather than pull back on the reins, Slocum let the horse run out its normally fiery temper and made up some ground in the process.

Throughout the ride, Slocum spent so much time looking through his field glasses that he felt as though they'd been glued to his face. Even after he'd picked out a good spot to camp that was mostly surrounded by trees and had a watering hole not too far away, he still gazed through the glasses, searching for any trace of the men he knew were tracking him.

"Find anything?" Eliza asked from the camp.

"Nope. They had to have found your horse by now, though, which means they know they've been duped."

"Or they might just figure they made a mistake."

"Either way leads to the same spot," Slocum said. "They'll be widening their search and looking under every rock to try and find us."

"Which will slow them up even more."

"Yeah," Slocum admitted. "I suppose that's right."

"Can we make a proper fire tonight?"

"Nothing too big, but I don't see the harm in cooking a real supper."

"Perfect!" Eliza said. "What will you be making?"

Slocum shook his head. "I get to crawl on my belly and cook dinner? I don't think you're paying me enough, lady."

"You'll change your mind once we get to Bray. You get a percentage, remember? I'll make more than enough to compensate you for hunting down a critter or two for us to eat."

"We can set up a small fire," Slocum told her. "That doesn't mean I'll announce our presence by firing off shots for those gunmen to hear."

"Aww," Eliza sighed as she stuck her lower lip out just enough for a cute little pout.

"We can warm up what we've already got," Slocum said. "It's either that or nothing."

"You're a hard man, John Slocum."

"You don't know the half of it," he told her.

Eliza's pout might have struck a chord with him, or Slocum could also have been distracted by the way Eliza sat with her legs curled up to one side while keeping her upper body propped up on one arm. The fact that she'd chosen to wear jeans that hugged the curves of her hips for the day's ride didn't hurt matters either.

As Slocum walked over to where Eliza was resting, he noticed her watching him intently. By the time he was in front of her, she was sitting upright and gazing up at him with wide, expectant eyes. "We do have some unfinished business, you know."

"Of course I do," she replied with a nod. Repositioning herself so she was on her knees, she let one hand stray along the front of her body so she could pull the top few buttons of her blouse loose along the way. "You mentioned that you'd earned a whole lot more than just a sip of water."

"Oh, yeah. I was thinking more along the lines of whiskey."

"I wasn't." With that, Eliza pulled her blouse open the rest of the way so it came loose from where it had been tucked into her jeans. She then reached out to take hold of Slocum's belt and worked the buckle until it gave way.

Slocum looked up and around as memories of what had happened the last time drifted through his head. Unlike the previous night, this camp was surrounded on three sides by enough trees and dry bushes to keep anyone or anything from creeping up on them. On the fourth side was the watering hole. Even if someone did get past Slocum's horse without causing the big fellow to stir, they would need to splash for a few steps before getting to the camp. When Slocum looked down again, he was just in time to see Eliza tug his pants down so she could get to his growing erection.

As if sensing his eyes upon her, Eliza looked up to stare directly into them as she opened her mouth and took Slocum's cock halfway inside. She closed her lips around him and slid her tongue along the bottom of his shaft as she devoured every last inch of him. Reaching up to hold onto his legs, Eliza hungrily sucked on him before he could make a sound.

Easing her head back, Eliza teased him with the tip of her tongue until his cock was so hard that he could barely stand it. "Jesus," Slocum said as he grabbed the back of Eliza's head and urged her to continue. She was only too happy to comply, and bobbed her head back and forth, again and again, as though he was her last meal.

"Hold on now," Slocum forced himself to say. "Not so fast, lady."

Eliza pouted again and looked up at him with wide eyes. She knew she was laying it on thick, but that somehow added to it when she whispered, "Did I do something wrong?"

All Slocum had to do was strip out of his shirt, kick off his boots, and pull off his jeans to get Eliza to follow suit. She wriggled her hips to allow her jeans to drop, and smiled eagerly as she did. Now that she was out of the rugged denim, her blouse flowed around her in the passing breeze. The sun had dipped below the horizon by the time they'd settled into camp, so now there was just enough light from the moon and stars to give her skin an inviting aura.

"You're doing everything right so far," Slocum said as he stepped forward to press his body against hers. Sliding his hands beneath her shirt, he slid his palms up and down along her sides before reaching around to cup her tight little backside. "Lay down and we'll see about keeping that lucky streak alive."

Excitement flashed in Eliza's eyes as she practically dropped to the ground and lay on her back. As Slocum settled on top of her, Eliza was more than willing to spread her

legs to accommodate him. Even though the tip of Slocum's
rod brushed against the moist spot between her thighs, he
didn't allow himself to enter her. Instead, he took hold of
one of her hands, pinned it to the ground, and lowered his
mouth to her breasts.

Eliza pulled in a shuddering breath and tried to watch
what Slocum was doing. He gently bit the skin above her
breasts, and then worked his way down to the pert mounds
of supple flesh. Slocum let his teeth move along her tit and
when his teeth brushed against her erect nipple, Eliza sucked
in another breath and arched her back so Slocum would take
more of her into his mouth.

"I need you inside me, John," Eliza whispered. "Don't
make me wait anymore."

With the sun down and the stars out, the air had taken on
a cool edge. Slocum wasn't cold by any means, and he
didn't even feel a chill once he was lying on top of Eliza and
had positioned himself so he was on the verge of entering
her. He lingered there for a few seconds, keeping his hard
cock nestled against the wet lips of her pussy. Feeling Eliza
squirm expectantly made him even harder, but it also made it
more difficult to hold back.

He finally pushed his hips forward and buried his cock all
the way inside her. Eliza let out a shaky breath and gripped
Slocum tightly in more ways than one. Her arms wrapped
around so she could dig her fingernails into his shoulder
blades. Her legs wrapped around his waist to pull him in,
and her pussy clenched him tightly as her entire body began
to tremble.

"Oh, God, John . . . oh, God."

Rather than start thrusting in and out of her, Slocum only
withdrew a little bit and waited there before driving back
inside her. Once he did bury himself within her again, he
ground his hips back and forth, side to side, until Eliza's
trembling caused her to press the back of her head against
the ground so she could ride out her climax to its conclusion.

Before long, Eliza's eyes came open and she chuckled

breathlessly. "That took me by surprise. A real nice surprise, though."

Slocum grinned and waited until it looked like Eliza was about to catch her breath. Before she could do that, he pumped his hips forward and then started thrusting in earnest. Eliza started to say something, but she didn't have the breath to form the words. She moved her hands down along his sides, but quickly reached out to grab hold of the ground beneath her as if she needed something to steady herself.

Although he hadn't told her as much, Slocum had been thinking about this for a good long while. From the moment he'd first laid eyes on Eliza's tall, lean body and admired the way her long black hair flowed over her shoulders, he was thinking about seeing what was under those skirts of hers. When he saw her in her riding clothes, he'd only wanted to peel her jeans away and explore every inch of her body.

The bit of time they'd had before didn't do him any good. That had just been a scrap when he'd wanted a whole meal. Now that he had her naked and spread out beneath him, he was going to relish every last second.

Eliza arched her back and clenched her eyes shut as if she was having an intense dream. Her arms stretched out to either side, and she flinched a bit when Slocum closed his hands over hers so he could pin them down against the earth. Although she continued to writhe and squirm, she didn't make any effort to pull her hands free. In fact, her body responded to it very nicely as another climax rippled just beneath her surface.

Rising up over her, Slocum pumped between her legs and let his eyes wander down along her naked body. Her breasts were small and pert, but stood out proudly when she arched her back. Her nipples were erect and begging to be sucked, but Slocum wasn't about to stop or even slow down to do so.

When he let go of her hands, Slocum saw a flicker of disappointment on Eliza's face. That flicker soon vanished when Slocum straightened up so he was kneeling between her legs. From there, Slocum grabbed her tight little ass in both hands, lifted her a bit off the ground, and pumped into her all over again.

"Oh, John," she groaned.

Grinning down at her, Slocum said, "You need to be quiet."

Eliza was about ready to make a comment to that, but was cut short when Slocum pulled her in close to him and drove every last inch of his cock into her. Eliza's eyes opened wide, and she closed them again as Slocum's thrusts took on a vigorous rhythm. She stretched out and sifted her fingers through her hair, spreading her legs open wide and allowing Slocum to drive her straight into another orgasm.

This time, Slocum didn't hold back in the slightest. He gripped her hips and reached around to feel the firm lines of her ass as he pumped into her again and again. Eliza climaxed a second time in a way that put the first to shame. Her entire body shook and she bit down on her lower lip to keep from screaming. Slocum had to fight to stay quiet himself as he plowed into her one last time before exploding within her.

Just when he thought he was spent, Slocum felt Eliza's pussy tightening around him and her hips wriggling back and forth within his grasp.

Slocum pulled out of her so he could lie down. "Damn, lady," he breathed. "That was . . ."

Eliza was shaking her head as she crawled forward and straddled him. "You're talking like it's over."

"Oh, it ain't over. I just need a second to collect myself."

"Here," she said as she reached between his legs and started stroking his limp cock. "Let me help." In a matter of seconds, he responded to her touch and started growing hard again. Once he was halfway there, Eliza positioned him between her legs so she could rub her wet pussy up and down against his length. "How's that? Better?"

Taking hold of her again, Slocum replied, "I believe so."

In short order, he was inside Eliza once more. This time, she sat astride him with her hands flat against his chest while grinding her hips in little circles. Slocum lay back, relaxed, and felt his erection returning bit by glorious bit. Even when he was harder than he'd been before, he just kept his hands on her strong thighs and felt her muscles work.

After a bit of rest and a quick supper, Slocum took the reins back and made Eliza feel like a lucky lady indeed.

13

Bray was a good-sized town on the eastern border of the Arizona Territory. Even though it had a good mix of merchants and entertainments of various sorts, the railroad hadn't seen fit to grace the town with its presence and that was never a good thing. There had been talk about railroad scouts disapproving of all the gambling in Bray, which led to the tracks being laid elsewhere. Whether that was true or not, the rumors kept spreading and the damage was done.

Then again, one merchant's damage is a few saloon owners' advantage. Word spread among the gamblers about Bray's predicament, causing several professionals to come see the town for themselves. A few games hosted by more than a few gracious saloons brought even more professional cardplayers and cheats alike. After that, Bray was known as a fine place to play for high stakes. To the rest of the territory, it was a town on its last legs and in the grips of lawlessness.

The arrangement worked out pretty well for all concerned.

The Cooking Fire was a restaurant on the corner of Wilson Avenue and Fifth Street. It was a little place that always smelled like boiling potatoes and bad coffee, but it did its share of steady business. Even if the customers stopped coming altogether, The Cooking Fire's doors wouldn't close. Armand Theil got enough use out of the place to justify keeping it in working order.

Theil was a lean fellow with close-set eyes and a thick head of light blond hair. His mouth resembled a thin line that had been sliced into a piece of limestone and was almost always curled at the corners to form a subtle, humorless smile. Always dressed in finery that couldn't be found in any of the little shops in Bray, Theil wore his money like a peacock showing its feathers. The resemblance ended there, however, since peacocks rarely wore nickel-plated .45s strapped under their wings.

Picking at a slice of pie at a table facing the front of the restaurant, Theil glanced up when he heard the bell over the front door ring. He recognized the two men that walked inside, but didn't acknowledge them. Instead, he shifted his shoulder holster to make sure Dawes and Mark knew it was there.

Both men approached Theil's table and waited for a greeting. When they didn't get it, or even an invitation to sit down, Dawes and Mark immediately started to get nervous.

"I know we're late, Mr. Theil," Dawes said. After taking a look around to find only a couple of customers in the place, he added, "It took a little longer than we thought."

Still nothing from Theil.

Mark's face was coated in trail dust, which made him look even more like a short stretch of rough road. Sniffing the air, he asked, "That shepherd's pie I smell?"

"Did you do what you were supposed to do?" Theil asked.

"We went to East Padre and found . . . uh . . . who we were supposed to find."

"Forget about them," Theil snapped as he waved a dismissive hand at the one table occupied by paying customers. "Look at me and tell me you got your job done. Is that bitch dead?"

Although they'd been content to mind their own business

before, Theil's words and vicious tone were enough to catch the customers' attention. They looked back at Theil's table, but quickly averted their eyes when they saw the armed men standing at it.

Dawes pulled out the other chair at Theil's table and Mark took one from another table for himself. As soon as he was sitting, Dawes said, "We got to where she was staying and would have killed her then and there, but someone stepped in on her behalf."

Even though Mark knew the facts for himself, he kept quiet and let Dawes tell the story however he saw fit. When Mark caught the server's attention, he signaled for him to bring over an order of the day's special. It was indeed shepherd's pie.

"Who stepped in?" Theil asked.

"Some gunfighter by the name of John Slocum," Dawes told him. "I think I heard of him and he's—"

"I don't give half a shit who he is. Did you kill her or not?"

Since Mark seemed content to stay turned around and watch the server talk to the cook about his order, Dawes shook his head and said, "Things got cocked up on account of this fellow she hired."

"Did you really go up against this man?" Theil asked as he narrowed his eyes as if he was inspecting a bug that had been trapped beneath a glass. "Or are you just covering your ass?"

"We went against him, all right. Andy's dead because of it."

"Who's Andy?"

"One of those two fellas that met us outside of East Padre," Dawes explained.

Suddenly, Theil's eyes widened and he said, "Oh, you mean the tracker that came so highly recommended?"

"Yes."

"I take it he wasn't worth his fee."

"He tracked them down just fine. Far as we could tell, he tried to make a move on his own and was killed."

"Wasn't just killed," Mark added. "Slaughtered is more like it."

Theil shifted some of his focus back to the pie in front of

him. "I thought he traveled with some other gunman. Edmonson was his name?"

"Like I said, Andy scouted ahead on his own. He must've thought he had a clear shot or . . ."

"Or he just got caught red-handed," Theil said as a way to fill the gap Dawes had left behind.

"Right," Dawes said. "I hear this Slocum fellow is real good, so it could have been either one."

"Sounds like he was making an example of that piss-poor scout," Theil pointed out. "But the bitch is still alive?"

"We took a shot at her at the saloon, but she got away from us. We tore apart the whole damn place and then tried gunning her down the next day."

"That's when Slocum stepped in?" Theil asked.

"Oh, yeah!" Mark said as he rubbed his hands together. Both of the other men at the table looked over at him, only to find that Mark was just getting worked up about the plate of food being set down in front of him. Seeing that he was being watched, Mark tucked a napkin under his collar and said, "You two go right ahead."

"Don't mind if we do," Theil said in a controlled tone of voice.

Before Theil could get angry or Mark could make even more of an ass of himself, Dawes continued with his report. "Slocum stepped in and warned us to stay away, but we went about our business. That was before we knew he was acting on her behalf, of course."

"Of course," Theil replied with a little less control in his voice.

"She and him skipped town and Andy rode ahead to track them down. When he didn't come back, we pieced together where he went and that's when we found him. Or . . . what was left of him."

One of Theil's eyebrows went up as if it had been attached to a string. "That sounds interesting. What was left exactly?"

"He was shot up pretty good. We wouldn't have known it was him apart from his fancy scabbard."

SLOCUM AND THE LUCKY LADY   135

Slowly nodding as if he was assessing the losses to his roof after a windstorm, Theil asked, "So what kept you busy the rest of the time? You were supposed to be back yesterday."

Dawes pulled in a breath that expanded his barrel chest like a set of bellows. When he looked over at Mark for some support, all he got was a halfhearted shrug and a belch. Choking back the urge to knock Mark onto his useless ass, Dawes said, "We picked up their trail on our own after we found Andy. The tracks led from one camp to another and then—"

"I don't need a full account," Theil interrupted. "Just answer my goddamned question."

"We only found one of their horses."

"Who was riding it?"

After a heavy pause, the big man said, "Nobody."

Theil nodded and placed the last piece of pie crust into his mouth. He then calmly set his fork down, pushed his plate aside, and drew his .45 from the rig under his left arm. "Give me one good reason why I shouldn't rid myself of you two right here and now."

To his credit, Dawes didn't show much more than a twitch after finding himself at the wrong end of Theil's gun. Judging by the look on his face, his predicament wasn't actually much of a surprise. "The first time we saw Slocum, we figured he was just some asshole checking on the shooting in the saloon where Banner was staying. The next time, we still couldn't be sure who he was or if he was on Banner's side. Now we know who he is and that him and Banner are close."

"How close?"

"If we got close enough to know that, we would'a shot them both, Mr. Theil."

Despite his curt nod, Theil didn't lower his pistol. "Fair enough. And so I'm to believe that Banner and her hired gun were also late in getting here?"

"We searched every inch of the trail that led here directly," Dawes explained. "They may have shaken us, but they had to have holed up somewhere or circled around for a longer ride."

"So," Theil grumbled as he sifted through the information

and ticked off all the possibilities in his head, "they're either behind you or may have gotten here at the same time since you men were apparently taking your time to look under every rock and in every cave."

"More or less," Mark said through a mouthful of shepherd's pie.

Tucking his pistol back into its holster, Theil said, "All right then. I didn't want Banner to make it here, but it sounds to me like you men did a good job of shaking her up. That could go a ways in rattling her at the tables."

"Yes, sir," Dawes replied.

"Needless to say, you men don't get the bonus I offered for cutting her off before getting to town."

Dawes winced when he heard that, and Mark swallowed his next bite as if he'd accidentally eaten a rock, but neither man was about to speak up against the ruling.

"But I've got another offer," Theil told them. "If this Slocum is the same man I've heard tell about, then he's a gunman of some repute. If you kill him, I'll double the bonus I was offering before."

That brought smiles to the two men's faces.

"But," Theil added as he raised a finger, "the job can't be done while we're playing. The men running these games are particular about keeping the peace at their tables. I'll even pay the standard bonus if you keep that bitch rattled enough that she can't focus on what she's doing while she plays. You men need to be seen and you need to keep whatever gunmen she's hired away from her so they can't help her or receive any orders. At the very least, you men need to discourage her from being in this town and make anyone else regret taking a fee from her. Folks must learn what happens when they land on my bad side."

"They'll know soon enough, Mr. Theil," Dawes assured him. "We'll see to that."

Slocum figured he'd approach the town using some run-down trail or footpath that led into Bray from an angle that wouldn't be watched. What he hadn't been expecting was to come at the town past a group of slaughterhouses and shabby stables.

"This place sure has gone to hell," Slocum said.

"For a gambler, it's the Promised Land," Eliza replied. "Just about every business around here caters to cardplayers. If you can't find a suitable game at one of the saloons or poker halls, there's a fine selection at any back room and even in a few alleys."

"I've had my fill of alleys for the time being," Slocum muttered.

Eliza proved her bravery by pulling in a deep breath and holding it in her lungs. Even though Slocum could only smell a mix of rotting food, manure, and human waste, she let out her breath as if she'd sampled a breeze that had come to her after blowing across a mountain stream. "I never thought I'd make it here, John. Theil told me I'd never see Bray again, and after I nearly got killed in that saloon back in East Padre, I was beginning to believe him."

"How close did they get to you back there?"

Slocum could feel her shudder in the saddle behind him.

"I'd rather not dwell on that," she replied. "We've got enough on our plate already. Theil may not exactly run this town, but he doesn't need to. If there is anyone wearing a badge around here, they're just collecting bribes from whoever can pay at the time. I've seen killings get settled by a bidding war to see who could get the sheriff and his deputies on their side. Whoever had the most money got to walk away a free man and whoever didn't was hauled off to a cage or strung up an hour later."

"Lawmen whoring themselves out, huh? Not too big of a surprise in a town with so much money flowing through it. I suppose it's just kind of hard to believe there's that much money around here."

Eliza kept smiling even as they passed dirty buildings that looked as if their foundations had been rotted by the sewage ditches flowing nearby. "It may not look like much, especially here, but Bray is a hell of a place. Just wait and you'll see."

A few minutes later, Slocum could see that Eliza was at least right about the town being better elsewhere. Having circled around to approach from the ass end of the place, Slocum now rode down one of Bray's main streets. The storefronts and saloons farther into the town were a lot more appealing than what he'd passed on the way in. The farther south he rode, the more Bray looked like the little mining town he remembered. Before too long, even the air smelled more of food being prepared and cigars being smoked.

As if sensing what Slocum was thinking, Eliza patted him on the shoulder and said, "See? I told you it wasn't so bad."

Slocum acknowledged her with half a nod, then pointed toward the brightly painted windows and signs marking the saloons splayed out in front of him. "Where were you planning on meeting up with Theil? If it's any of these places, we should probably double back. I'd rather get settled in somewhere before getting into another scrape."

"Take your next left," Eliza told him. "There are some hotels that way, and one of them even sells some nice clothes."

"We're not here to shop," Slocum scolded. "Besides, with all the dresses and such we're hauling, you should have plenty to wear."

"Do you have any formal clothes or just more of the same?"

Twisting around to look at her, he asked, "Me? What the hell difference do my clothes make?"

"Just because this isn't San Francisco doesn't mean we have to look like savages. Do you want to stick out like a sore thumb?"

"No. And from what I've seen so far, I don't look any worse than the rest of the dregs around here."

"Out here maybe," Eliza said. "But not all of these places cater to cowboys and vagrants. They toss them out on their ears. Unless you'd prefer to draw attention to yourself, I'd suggest you at least buy a nice jacket."

Slocum looked down at himself. Although he wasn't about to admit she was completely right, he was covered with plenty of dust and smelled less like a man and more like the horse he'd ridden for the last several days. "I suppose I could do that if you think it would help."

Patting him once again on the shoulder, Eliza said, "It would help tremendously." After a slight pause, she added, "You know what else would help? A bath."

Slocum pulled his reins to steer his horse to the left. "Only if you join me."

"Are you calling me dirty?"

"That depends on how you behave once we're in the tub."

14

When he entered the clothing store around the corner from the hotel, Slocum was expecting to find bundles of wares that had fallen off the back of a wagon while on their way to greener pastures. What he found was a modest tailor in his late fifties who only knew a handful of English phrases, which he peppered in among his native Greek. Slocum picked out a black suit coat and a pair of dark gray trousers to go along with it. Eliza approved heartily, and the Greek tailor made some quick alterations so Slocum could walk out as a new man.

"You sure you don't want to finish the outfit?" Eliza asked.

"I don't mind these things," Slocum said as he fussed with the sleeves of his coat and then placed his watch in his vest pocket so the chain crossed his midsection. "I'm not about to bother breaking in a new hat and boots just to impress your gambler friends."

Although she frowned at first, Eliza could tell when her pouting lip was working and when it wasn't. This time it wasn't, and she settled for dusting off the hat on Slocum's head. "I guess this'll do."

"Yes, it will. Now where is Theil? After hearing so much about this asshole, I'd like to get a look at him for myself."

"No need to hurry," Eliza said as she snaked her arm around Slocum's. "I'm sure he'll find us soon enough. Besides, it'll be more fun that way."

Slocum didn't think his definition of fun matched Eliza's, but he tucked the bundle of his old clothes under his arm and walked with her back to their hotel. They only stopped in long enough for him to drop off his clothes at the front desk and set down enough money to cover the expense of getting them washed.

"You'll have them by tomorrow," the clerk assured him.

"Keep them if you like," Eliza said. "Or better yet, burn them. We'll win more than enough to make up for it."

Although Slocum rolled his eyes at that, the clerk smiled and put the bundle under his desk. After that, Eliza strolled beside him down the street as if she was enjoying a picnic.

Even if the owners of Bray's many gambling establishments weren't very creative in naming their places, they did have a good sense of irony. The Straight Deal Poker Hall was, as near as Slocum could figure, smack in the middle of town. Surrounded by saloons and other gambling dens on all sides, Slocum and Eliza passed more than a few whorethouses between the Straight Deal and the hotel Eliza had chosen. It seemed that Bray truly did know how to attract its particular brand of guest. The working girls sat on the porches or in the whorehouse windows, but kept from calling out or exposing themselves like they might in any old cow town. Instead, the girls watched every step Slocum took as he was led to the Straight Deal.

"This place isn't as rowdy as I would have imagined," he said.

"Don't get too comfortable just yet," Eliza replied. "Why don't you let me go inside first and then you can come in after a minute or so?"

Normally, Slocum would have prefered to keep her in sight the entire time. But since this was her show, he shrugged and allowed her to disentangle from his arm. "You find any trouble, just holler."

Patting his cheek, she said, "I'll scream bloody murder."

Oddly enough, Eliza gave those words a playful quality. She pulled open the doors and stepped inside, leaving Slocum alone on the street.

Of course, compared to the desolate trail that had brought him there, Slocum was hardly alone. There were folks on both sides of the street, and plenty more could be heard within the various establishments. Taking his pouch from inside his pocket, he set about rolling himself a cigarette as he leaned against a post outside the Straight Deal. Even though Slocum had used his tobacco mostly to mark where he'd been, there was no denying it was fine in quality. Once he was done rolling the cigarette, he fished into his pocket for his tin of lucifers. The spark flared up, but it wasn't late enough in the day for that to draw much attention to his face. He touched the sputtering flame to the end of his cigarette, pulled in a lungful of fragrant smoke, and then expelled it through his nostrils.

As he savored the cigarette, Slocum let his eyes wander from one face to another. It was easy enough to spot the gamblers. They were the ones sizing up everyone else like mountain lions searching for the weakest members of a herd. In the town of Bray, the mountain lions were forced to shift their gaze to one another if they meant to survive.

In the amount of time it took him to smoke that cigarette down to a nub, Slocum had heard three different songs being played upon three different instruments, a few shouting matches, as well as a couple of rowdy moans from one of the nearby whorehouses. Even after one of the fights ended with a man getting tossed out through a set of batwing doors, not one lawman made his presence known.

"This may not be such a bad place after all," Slocum muttered to himself.

He turned around and walked toward the front doors of the Straight Deal. Since those were normal double doors and set next to a front window that had been all but painted over, Slocum couldn't see much of what was going on inside the place. There hadn't been any commotion of the violent sort coming from there, so he took his time and meandered inside without announcing his presence.

The Straight Deal Poker Hall was similar to most saloons, apart from the fact that there was no stage. The bar was to Slocum's right and stretched all the way to the other wall, rounded the corner, and then took up a good portion of that adjoining wall. The men that were at the bar leaned their backs against it so they could watch what was happening at any of the two dozen or so tables taking up most of the main floor. Not all of those tables were full, but there was more than enough going on to keep any spectator busy.

Slocum wasn't interested in just any game, however. The longer he went without catching sight of Eliza, the more uncomfortable he got. After taking a few more steps into the place so he could look for her, Slocum felt a bear's paw drop onto his shoulder that prevented him from moving another inch.

"You heeled?" a gruff voice asked.

Turning to get a look at who'd asked that question, Slocum discovered that the bear claw on his shoulder was attached to a bear of a man. While he had plenty of meat on his bones, the man was hardly fat. He filled out a suit that might very well have come from the same Greek tailor that Slocum had visited, but must have required double the material to cover his burly frame. The ring on the man's finger was big enough for Slocum to feel it knock against his shoulder blade.

"Is there a law against wearing your gun around here?" Slocum asked.

"No," the burly man growled as he flipped open Slocum's coat with a brush of his finger. "I just gotta know who to watch."

"Then you must have to watch every man in here."

"Yeah, but I know most of them. I don't know you."

Rather than give the burly man a reason to snap him like a twig, Slocum plastered a crooked smile onto his face and extended his right hand. "My name's John."

For a second, the hulking man looked down at Slocum's

hand as if he couldn't decide whether he wanted to shake it or rip it off. He decided upon the former and said, "Folks call me Grizzly."

"That's about right. I thought a bear was attacking me when you stopped me."

"Yeah," Grizzly said without even smiling at Slocum's clumsy delivery of that bad joke. "I hear that a lot."

"So now we know each other. Mind if I go in and have a drink?"

Grizzly wasn't through shaking Slocum's hand. In fact, he tightened his grip until some of the bones in that hand scraped against one another. "Leave your gun with me."

"What happens if I need it?" Slocum asked.

"Me or one of my boys will keep an eye on you. You won't need your gun."

As he let out a measured breath, Slocum took stock of everything else he was carrying. Apart from his Colt Navy, he had a slender knife in his boot as well as the knife he'd taken from Andy tucked under his belt at the small of his back. He had another pistol to replace the one Grizzly was demanding, but that was back in his hotel room.

"All right," Slocum said, knowing full well that he didn't have any other choice. "But I'd better get it back."

"You will."

Once his hand was released, Slocum denied the reflex to shake some feeling back into his fingers. Instead of giving Grizzly the satisfaction of seeing that, Slocum held the Colt around the cylinder and trigger guard so he could lift it from its holster without ruffling any feathers. When Grizzly took the gun from him, the big man's hand nearly enveloped the pistol completely. Letting his gun go like that made Slocum feel as if his fur was being brushed the wrong way. It didn't feel right and it grated on his nerves. Even though he'd let the gun go more or less voluntarily, he still thought of all the things he could do to Grizzly if he needed to take his weapon back by force.

To be honest, that list really wasn't too long.

"If I come back here, do I need to go through this again?" Slocum asked while trying to keep his voice friendly.

Grizzly shifted his hands and clasped them across his front, which made it difficult to tell whether he was still holding the Colt or if he'd slipped it into a pocket somewhere. "Once I know you, you can come and go as you like. But if you cause trouble, it won't matter if I know you or not. You'll wish you were never born."

Some men spat out their threats like they were forcing their fist through a wall. Men like Grizzly merely had to state them as plain facts. Slocum took the words to heart, knowing that Grizzly had the means to back them up.

"If any trouble gets started in here, it won't be on my account," Slocum said.

"Good. You can go on in now."

Taking that as the spoken equivolent of a boot to the backside, Slocum walked away from Grizzly and headed for the bar. It still irked him that his holster was empty, but he was there to check in on Eliza and he couldn't do that if he was tossed out by the monster guarding the front door.

As he approached the end of the bar that was closest to the door, Slocum looked around at the tables taking up the rest of the room. There were plenty of games being played and plenty of attractive women sitting at or walking among the tables. The first thing that came to Slocum's mind was that Eliza was right. Any man who walked in there looking like a cowpoke would have stuck out like a sore thumb.

"Fix you up with a drink?"

Slocum turned toward the voice and found a skinny fellow that looked to be right around his age. The bartender had a long, clean-shaven face and scruffy brown hair that was cut short enough to look more like bristles sprouting from his scalp. "I see you met Grizzly," the bartender said.

"Yeah and I don't think I made a good impression."

"Don't worry none. The men that Grizzly don't like wind up making a real good impression on the floor, if you catch my meaning. How about a drink to soothe your nerves?"

"My nerves are fine, but I'll still take the drink. Make it a whiskey."

The barkeep turned and picked out a bottle from the rack behind him. After he'd selected the right one, he poured a healthy shot into a glass and set it down on the bar. "You here for the tournament or just looking for a game?"

"Tournament?" Slocum asked as a way to test the waters.

"Well, not an official tournament as such, but the players have arranged to come to town and see how much they can swindle from each other." Suddenly, the barkeep's face dropped and he added, "Not that there's cheating here! I mean, the games we run are—"

Slocum put the glass to his mouth and tipped his head back to send the whiskey down. It was like smooth fire that immediately put a smile on his face. "Relax," he told the barkeep. "I know what you mean."

"Oh, good. You need anything, you can ask for me. Want to know about any games being played here or in our back room? You just ask for Sid."

"I've got a question for you, Sid. Have you seen a woman walk in here not too long ago? Dark hair and she's wearing a dark red dress."

"Tall lady? Hair that went all the way down to her . . . well . . . long hair?"

"That's the one," Slocum said.

Sid stretched his back and craned his neck like a turtle trying to get a better look from its shell. "She came in here a few minutes ago and met up with Mr. Theil. He usually plays at one of the back tables."

Slocum looked at the back of the room. When he couldn't find her, he started looking at all the tables in the rear section of the hall. He still came up empty. "Did you say something about back rooms?"

"Yes," Sid replied as he snapped his fingers. "Mr. Theil plays back there as well. I don't think he left, so he's probably back there. I can check, if you like."

"No bother. I can have a look for myself."

Sid winced and explained, "You can't just walk back there. That's why the tables are back there instead of out here. I'd be happy to see if Mr. Theil is back there. Do you think he'll know where to find your lady friend?"

"If Theil's back there, she'll be with him."

Placing his hands flat upon the bar, Sid hopped up and swung his legs over the polished wooden surface. He hit the floor like a cat and straightened his apron before looking at Slocum and saying, "I'll just run back there and check."

Before Sid could make a move, Slocum grabbed his arm and said, "Don't say anything to Theil. Just tell me if they're back there."

"Someone has to vouch for you, sir."

"Then ask the lady and be quiet about it."

"Oh, of course," Sid said confidently. "I'll be very discreet. What's your name?"

"John."

"John it is. I won't be a minute."

Even though the room was pretty large and Slocum didn't know how much space was behind closed doors, Sid moved fast enough to make good on his promise. The barkeep nodded and waved to players and working girls alike as he sped through the room as though the floor had been greased beneath him. After disappearing through a set of double doors that were guarded by two men, Sid soon came out and retraced his steps.

When he got back to Slocum, Sid was hardly even breathing hard. "She's back there, John, and she says you can come on back."

"Much obliged."

Sid hopped over the bar and didn't lose a step before asking, "You want another whiskey to take back there with you?"

"Don't mind if I do."

The whiskey was poured and Slocum put some money on the bar before Sid had to explain that the first round was on the house. "Keep the change," Slocum said.

"Will do! Like I said before . . . you need anything, you ask for Sid!"

Slocum was concerned about finding Eliza after losing sight of her for too long. Before he could think about that, he had to contend with the pair of apes guarding the private card tables.

Even though neither of the two guards could have stood toe to toe with Grizzly, they wore their guns for all to see. Even without those pistols, the men had fists that looked like petrified stumps. Slocum walked right up to them and looked each man in the eyes, one after the other. Neither of the guards said a word, but they stepped aside without a fuss after a quick glance at Sid.

Compared to the rest of the place, the back room felt like a coffin. Dark paper on the walls and fancy rugs on the floor cut every sound down to a whisper. Beyond the double doors, there was only a short hallway that had one door on either side and a third door at the far end. Both doors along the hallway were open, but voices were only coming from one of those rooms. He walked up to the room on the left and stopped so he could get a look inside before entering.

"Evening, Mr. Slocum," said a man who sat with his back to the wall so he could face the doorway. "I'm Armand Theil. Miss Banner and I were just having a conversation."

Since there was no use in hiding, Slocum stepped into the doorway so he could at least get a look at what he was up against.

He didn't like what he saw.

15

Theil sat facing the doorway with a card table between himself and Slocum. Eliza sat to Theil's left, with a man on either side of her. Slocum recognized one of those men as Dawes, but the other one didn't look familiar. Both of those two had their arms draped around Eliza's shoulders to keep her from moving. There were two others in the room, leaving one notable exception.

"Where's Lem?" Slocum asked. "Skulking behind a wall somewhere, waiting to get a clean shot at my back?"

Theil smiled and let one eyebrow flicker up and down. "I think I've got more than enough muscle in this room without Lem's help. Why don't you have a seat?"

Slocum didn't move toward any of the chairs. He looked over at Eliza and studied her for any sign that she'd been hurt.

"They got to me the second I walked in and wouldn't let me say anything to Sid," Eliza said in a rush. "This is usually a safe place to play. Neutral territory. At least it was until this snake in the grass hired an army to protect himself against a woman."

Still grinning like he was holding every ace in the deck, Theil shrugged dramatically and said, "What can I say to that? You do seem to have a point. Then again, considering the penalty for cheating around here, I'd say that even the owner of this fine establishment would be in my corner."

"So all the guards in this place are yours?" Slocum asked.

"Just the men in this room," Eliza cut in before she was silenced by a quick left-handed slap from Dawes. As soon as she could snap her face back around, Eliza spat, "This prick isn't going to scare me away from here! I don't care how many strutting assholes are on his payroll."

Dawes pulled his arm back to deliver a quick jab to the side of her face. His punch wasn't delivered with full power, but it came quickly enough to land before anyone could do anything to stop it.

Slocum's hand went reflexively for his cross-draw holster. "Are you all right, Eliza?" he asked.

Dabbing at her mouth with the back of one hand, she wiped away a trickle of blood and nodded.

"Save the posturing," Theil said. "I know damn well you were disarmed before you got into this place."

"What the hell is this about?" Slocum asked. "You must know by now that we're not carrying enough money to make all this trouble worth your while.

"This is a friendly warning," Theil said. "Miss Banner knows what she's done and she knows she still has to answer for it. I'm willing to pull her aside right now and show her the lay of the land. This way, things are a lot less messy and nobody has a reason to leave town before playing some poker. If she refrains from playing in these games and thinning out my winnings, I'll let the matter drop. Of course, she'll still have to pay me that money she owes me, but I'll leave her healthy enough to earn a living once she does."

Eliza squirmed beneath the arms of the men on either side of her. "I don't have your money."

"I know that," Theil shot back. "Why do you think you're still alive right now? As for that one," he said while shifting his eyes toward Slocum, "I don't know if I approve of you bringing in a hired gun like that. It sullies the spirit of the game."

Meeting Theil's smug grin with one of his own, Slocum lowered the hand that had been reaching for the empty holster. "You gave your warning, and I'm guessing you got the one I sent to you?"

Theil's grin was barely tarnished as he said, "I don't believe I know what you're referring to."

"Sure you do," Slocum said as he eased his right hand back under his coat. "Just ask the man who used to carry this."

The second those words were out, Slocum reached all the way around to grab the knife he'd been keeping at the small of his back. In a quick, fluid motion, he snapped his arm forward and sent the knife flying across the room. The blade turned once through the air and then stuck into Dawes's arm with a solid *thunk*. It was the same arm he'd used to hit Eliza.

Everyone but Dawes jumped to their feet. Theil hopped up and put his back to the wall while three of his men rushed toward the door. Eliza took advantage of the opening she'd been given by twisting away from the arms keeping her in her chair. Since Dawes was trying to pull the knife out of his arm, he didn't have any objection to letting go of her. Once she was up and out of her chair, Eliza circled around to Theil's side of the table.

Slocum then gained a bit of an edge by doing something the other men hadn't been expecting. He moved into the room instead of retreating from the superior numbers. More than that, Slocum charged straight toward the first man he could see that had a weapon handy. That man just happened to be Dawes, and the weapon was the knife sticking out of him.

As the other two raced around the table to get to him, Slocum dove toward Dawes, slapped the big man's hand away from the handle of the knife, and then ripped it free. He made sure to give the knife a twist before ripping it loose. That way, Slocum put Dawes completely out of the fight.

"What did I tell you men, goddamn it?" Theil snarled as he pulled his .45 from its holster.

Slocum noticed the gunmen were hesitant to show their guns. Now that Theil even seemed slow to pull his trigger, Slocum's theory was proven beyond a doubt. Before he could get to Theil, however, Eliza got to him first.

She lashed out with her fingernails as if they were claws and opened a few bloody gashes across Theil's face. Theil tried to push her away, but she had momentum on her side and merely rolled off his flailing arms and came at him again.

The gunmen outside this room weren't on Theil's payroll. Slocum had guessed that at first, but now he knew it for certain. If Theil and those men weren't afraid of getting on the bad side of Grizzly and the other watchdogs in the place, they would have opened fire long ago. Not only did this give Slocum an idea, but it gave him some breathing room in which to put that idea into motion.

Slocum pushed Dawes over, chair and all, and then hopped over the big man. Even though he was fairly certain the men didn't intend on pulling their triggers, he wasn't about to bet his life on them holding back forever. He lowered his shoulder and drove it into the second gunman who'd been holding Eliza in her chair. That man hit the wall and let out all the air from his lungs in a loud, wheezing grunt. From there, Slocum ran toward Eliza and wrapped an arm around her waist to haul her off her feet as she continued to kick and swing at Theil.

"Put me down, asshole!" Eliza growled without even looking back to see who'd picked her up.

Twisting himself around so Eliza was away from Theil, Slocum brought the bloody blade of Andy's knife to Theil's neck. "You know what happened to the man that carried this knife," Slocum said. "You had to have been told by now."

Of the two remaining gunmen, only one had made it around the table to confront Slocum. The other backed against a wall, holding a gun in each hand. When the overly eager gunman tried to get even closer to him, Slocum pushed the blade up a bit further under Theil's chin.

"Call off your dogs or I'll cut your damn head off," Slocum warned.

Theil nodded, but winced as he scraped his chin against the knife.

The gunman who'd been slammed against the wall was still collecting his breath. Dawes was grabbing onto his arm to keep the blood from spilling out of his wound. The gunman who'd raced halfway around the table froze in his tracks, and the man holding two guns kept his back to the opposite wall.

Feeling the blade push up into his neck a little more, Theil croaked, "Lower your guns. All of you." His eyes darted toward Slocum as a shaky smile made its way onto his face. "See? They weren't going to shoot, Mr. Slocum. We just wanted to deliver a message."

"I got your message, now you'll get mine. Your men are real good at shooting windows and kicking in doors, but I'm real good at sending loudmouthed assholes to a shallow grave. You and Eliza are here to play cards, so play cards. Whoever wins or loses will be decided by you two. If you try to stack the deck by putting a scare into her or hurt even the tip of one of her fingers, I'll take this knife or anything else I can get my hands on and bury it up your ass. Then I'll make a mess out of you or anyone else that steps out of line just like I made a mess out of the scout your boys sent after us. Got it?"

Theil seemed to be growing comfortable having the blade under his chin, because he looked at Slocum and asked, "You sweet on her, Mr. Slocum? She's a cheat, you know."

"Then take it up with the law or catch her in the act so she can be called out proper."

"You *are* sweet on her."

Although he kept his eyes more or less pointed at Theil, he kept watch on the rest of the men by using the edges of his vision. He might not have been able to see details, but he could sure as hell see one overly anxious gunman raising his arm to sight along the top of his pistol.

Slocum looked over at the anxious gunman, found the man taking aim at him, and then threw Andy's knife into the gunman's chest. The gunman's entire body jerked when the blade sank into him, causing him to pull his trigger and send a wild shot into Dawes's left shin. As Dawes grunted in pain, Slocum reached out to snag Theil's nickel-plated .45 away from him.

The gunman with the knife in his chest hit the floor on his knees at about the same time that Slocum fired a shot into the ceiling using Theil's gun. Slocum grinned when he heard the pounding of footsteps rushing toward the back room, and then tossed Theil's gun onto the table.

"For Christ's sake, Edmonson!" Theil snapped. "Put those damn guns away!"

Edmonson kept his back to the wall as he lowered both of his guns. The big fellows that had been guarding the double doors rushed into the room. One of them carried a .44 with at least two more pistols strapped under his arms and around his waist. The second guard held a sawed-off shotgun.

"Who fired those shots?" the guard with the pistol asked. "You were told no shooting! Throw all the fists you want, but no fucking shots!"

"Just a little disagreement," Theil replied as he held out his hands to show they were empty. "It's under control now."

"What happened to your neck?" Looking down at the gunman on the floor with a knife in his chest, the guard asked, "And what happened to him?"

"He was cheating," Theil said. "We caught him and he took a shot or two at me before we could put him down."

Both of the guards took in the sights without a lick of emotion on their faces. In the space of that stony silence, Slocum figured it was even money if those two would assess a fine for damages or just open fire to clean out every living thing in that room.

"You know the rules," the guard with the shotgun said. "You fire a gun in here and there better be a damn good reason."

"I told you. That man cheated. Is that tolerated here?"

"No."

"I didn't think so," Theil said.

"What about your neck? Or that man over there," the guard asked as he found Dawes. "Explain or we cut our losses right here and now."

Slocum stepped in by saying, "It's just like the man said. That one cheated and there was a scuffle. We tried to handle it, but things got out of control." Not only did Slocum see the guard with the shotgun looking at him, he could feel the man's gaze sink into him. Carefully, Slocum eased open his coat to show his holster. "See? Still empty."

The guard must have been confident in Grizzly's ability to sniff out guns because he said, "Then you can go."

Slocum held out a hand toward Eliza and she accepted it. Leading her past the guards, Slocum kept every last muscle in his body tensed for a fight in case the tempers inside that room took a turn for the worse. The guards only moved enough to let them pass, however, and they stepped back to seal off the room better than the door to a bank vault once Slocum and Eliza were gone.

"We didn't think we needed to remind you of the rules around here, Mr. Theil," one of the guards said.

Theil had a sputtering response to that, but Slocum was already too far down the hall to hear it. Eliza tugged on his hand as if she wanted to stay and watch the others squirm, but Slocum kept both of them moving. "Come on," he said. "I want to have a word with you."

16

Once they were outside, Slocum released his grip on Eliza's hand and asked, "What the hell was the meaning of that?"

She rubbed her hand and glared at him with a mix of anger and surprise. "Maybe you should ask Theil. He's the one that nearly killed me!"

"And you're the one that let him do it!"

"What?"

"You heard me!" Slocum snapped. "You were supposed to stay out where I could find you, not go off into a back room with the same man that's been trying to kill you. I don't mind taking the job of looking after you, but if you're going to make it that easy for Theil, I might as well save myself some grief and just ride out of here right now!"

Pulling her hands apart as if she was getting ready to take a swing at him, Eliza stood toe-to-toe with Slocum. Only at the last minute did she ease back a step and take a look around. The people on the street had matters of their own to contend with, but more than a few of them were taking notice of her and Slocum's heated discussion. Forcing herself to lower her voice, Eliza whispered, "It's good to know you were worried, but that was all a part of the plan."

"Plan?" Slocum asked in a voice that was just as low as

hers. Unfortunately, his next question wasn't so quiet. "That was part of a *plan*?"

Eliza grabbed Slocum's hand and pulled him away from the front of the Straight Deal. "Come along and I'll—"

"You'll what?" Slocum asked as he pulled his hand free. "Try to tell me you meant to almost get yourself killed? And don't try to pull me around like some goddamn kid!"

"Theil needed to think he was in control."

"It sure looked like he was in control to me! Are you about to tell me you were moments away from getting out of there before I showed up?"

"No," Eliza said, "but I was confident that you would show up. Besides, Theil wouldn't have killed me in there. Not when he'd already heard that I hired you and not before he got the money he was after."

"Are you sure about that?" Slocum asked. "Those men seemed more intent on killing you in East Padre and along the trail to this place."

"Theil doesn't want me here because he knows I can bust him in front of all these other gamblers. Since I'm here, he'll be after my money."

"You never answered my question," Slocum said evenly. "Are you sure about that?"

Eliza's mouth moved as if she meant to answer him right away. But it only took half a second of consideration for her to shake her head and tell him, "No. It was a gamble, but I knew he would have to take me somewhere else if he wanted things to get too messy. I was biding my time until you showed up. You were late by the way."

As frustrated as he was, Slocum had to chuckle at that. "Late, huh? You've got some real brass, you know that?"

Accepting that as a compliment, Eliza smirked. "So you keep telling me."

"How were you biding your time exactly?"

"I was trying to strike a partnership with Theil. He wasn't having any of it, but he liked the way I was asking."

Slocum knew all too well how convincing Eliza could be.

If anything, this very moment was a prime example. If she was a man, Slocum would have punched Eliza in the face and been done with it. A lot of women couldn't even get away with leading him around by the nose like that. Eliza Banner, on the other hand, wasn't just any other woman and she sure as hell wasn't a man.

"You've got to believe me, John. I'm not a fool who would just skip away to a back room with someone who wanted to kill her. The important thing is for Theil to think that's what I am."

"How do I know you're not leading me around right now?" Slocum asked. "How do I know you didn't strike up some arrangement with Theil and now you're just feeding me some sort of line so I'll keep going along with you?"

"Easy," Eliza replied with a casual shrug. "What would I have to gain by that? What could you offer to me that can top what I can get from beating Theil? I need you to trust me so this plan will work. If it does and I get over on Theil just for one or two big pots, I'll walk away from that table a rich woman and then I'll split it with you.

"If I set you up so I can double-cross you, what would it bring me?" she asked. "You'd be cross at me and maybe even want to kill me for doing something like that."

If anything, Slocum was at least confident that Eliza knew the score as far as that was concerned.

"Besides," she added, "if I had worked out a scheme with Theil, what the hell would I need you for at all?"

Slocum took a moment to think that through. It turned out that single moment was twice as much time as he needed. Rather than give her the pleasure of conceding the point so quickly, however, Slocum let her sweat it out for a few more seconds. Finally, he said, "All right, so you had a plan. It was a stupid plan, but I'll grant you that the plan was there."

"All right," Eliza said.

"Just tell me once more what the point of that plan was."

Eliza grinned as if she was about to rub her hands together and cackle like a scheming witch from a children's story. "It let Theil know I was in town and that I was through running and hiding like I have been for too long. It let him think he could get over on me anytime he wanted, and then it finally showed that you were truly on my side and that you could trump whatever card he decided to play back there as far as those hired assholes of his are concerned. Now Theil's nervous and he's got to be losing faith in his own men. When he plays, he'll be angry as hell and a little desperate."

"Prime pickings," Slocum had to admit.

Eliza nodded. "Prime indeed."

"I could have thought of a better way to do those things if you would have just let me know what you meant to do," Slocum said.

"Actually, I kind of made it all up as I was walking into the Straight Deal."

Slocum's eyes widened and he let out a slow whistle. "You made that up as you went?"

"I sure did," she said proudly.

"Well, that explains a lot."

"You're impressed with me, John. Admit it."

"I don't know if impressed is the word, but you're making me believe a bit more in luck." Slocum would never have told her as much, but he was damn impressed with someone who could come up with a harebrained idea like that and follow it through. He knew she had to have had at least one or two aces up her sleeve that she wasn't talking about, but he let her have them. After all, she was paying him and she could call her own shots.

"Before I lift another finger to help you, I'm going to need some assurance," he announced.

"What kind of assurance?"

"Something to show you trust me. I want to know where this money is that Theil's after. And if you tell me there is no money, I'm walking out of here this instant."

"There's money," she replied. "Plenty of it. I just don't have it on me."

"Close enough to the wrong answer. Good-bye, Eliza."

Grabbing Slocum's arm, she spoke in a quick whisper. "I had it sent ahead to the Straight Deal so I could draw from it when I got here."

Slocum studied her for any sign that she was lying. He knew that gambling was close to lying as a trade, but he'd been around her long enough to know how she looked when she was scared or worried. He also knew she was making sense. Sending a large sum of money to a gambling hall wasn't normally a smart thing to do, but the Straight Deal was safer than plenty of banks Slocum had visited. Her money being there would also explain why Eliza was so dead set on going there instead of locking horns with Theil over a card table in some other town.

"I also want an advance on my payment," Slocum said.

Eliza's eyebrows raised a bit when she heard that. "What?"

"You heard me. If you insist on going off half-cocked like you did back there, I'll want to turn some profit before you get yourself killed."

Her smile returned and she wrapped her arm around his. "Fair enough. How's a thousand sound?"

"You have that much on you?"

"It'll come out of my bankroll, but with the ground I gained in there, I should be able to make it up before too long. Come back with me to the hotel and I'll get it for you. While we're there . . ."

Slocum shook his head and planted his feet before she could drag him anywhere else. "Didn't you say the money was sent ahead to the Straight Deal?"

"There might be some in my room," she told him while batting her eyelashes. "Don't you believe me?"

"No. I don't."

"All right, but don't we have time for a quick . . . ?"

"No," Slocum said, even though it pained him to do so. "You carried out your plan, so now's the best time to follow through on it. Besides, I'm not about to let my guard down when most of my weapons are still inside that saloon."

Sticking her lip out in a pout, Eliza tugged on his arm

again. When she felt that he wasn't going to budge, she groaned, "Fine. Just don't think I'm letting you off the hook that easy, John Slocum."

This time, Slocum and Eliza walked into the Straight Deal Poker Hall together. Both of them were stopped by the big man at the front door.

"You didn't go fetch any more weapons, did you?" Grizzly asked.

Holding open his new coat, Slocum replied, "See for yourself."

Grizzly patted Slocum down roughly enough to rattle his back teeth. When the doorman was through, he shifted his focus to Eliza. Under most circumstances, the big man's hands touching her from head to toe might have been a bit too familiar. But there was no mistaking Grizzly's intentions. He was looking for something under her clothes, but he didn't seem too pleased when he found it.

"What's this?" Grizzly asked as he held what he'd found in the palm of his hand.

Eliza looked at the derringer as if she'd never seen it before. In Grizzly's hand, the gun looked more like a toy. "I've never had a problem carrying that before."

"You ain't allowed to carry guns in here. Neither of you."

"What about Mr. Theil?" Slocum asked.

"After what happened before, he ain't allowed to bring guns in here either," Grizzly replied.

"And his men?"

Grizzly shook his head gravely.

"I suppose you can enforce that?" Eliza asked. When she saw the look she got from Grizzly, Eliza immediately recoiled.

"You think I ain't good at what I do?" Grizzly snarled.

"Oh, no," Eliza stammered. "I wouldn't suggest such a thing."

While Slocum didn't usually take to seeing anyone push around a woman, he had to admit it was good to see someone able to back this particular woman down a notch or two. Once he'd had his fill, he interrupted by asking, "Are Theil and his men still inside?"

"The big games are in the main room from now on," Grizzly said. "After what happened, ain't nobody being allowed to play at the private tables. Too many gamblers in one place to take any more chances."

"Sounds good. Can we go now?"

Grizzly looked both of them over one last time and then nodded. "Yeah. But if you cause any more trouble . . ."

"We won't cause a bit of trouble," Slocum said. "We didn't cause any of it in the first place. But what happens if Theil causes trouble? What if he or his men get to a gun? I won't be able to defend myself."

"Don't worry about that. I can do my damn job."

Slocum didn't waver in the slightest when Grizzly attempted to stare him down. In fact, he returned the bigger man's glare with one of his own that was enough to give Grizzly something to think about. "You just be sure to stay on top of your job," Slocum warned. "Otherwise, things are bound to get messy."

Grizzly nodded and folded his thick arms across his massive chest. He didn't keep them from walking into the poker hall's main room and he didn't try to impose himself on either Slocum or Eliza. After the other two had walked away, Grizzly stepped back and waited to harass the next gambler that tried to get inside. He didn't have to wait long, since the place was quickly filling up.

Eliza stopped at the perimeter of the card tables and looked around like a general surveying the battlefield. "I see a lot of familiar faces."

When Slocum looked around, he spotted one or two gamblers that he might have seen elsewhere, but not enough to make him sit up and take notice. "Good, because I don't."

"Let's just hope they don't recognize you. Come on."

"No," Slocum said.

She stopped and whipped her head around as if she'd

been told that he was about to sprout a tail. "What? Why not?"

"You already proved that you can play poker," he said. "I believe in you enough to let you go and do your part. If I'm to keep you around long enough to do any damage to Theil's bankroll, I need room to maneuver."

"And what we talked about? About us being a team at the table?"

"I'll take my advance now and the rest will come later. You'll know when I expect to get it."

"I'll go see the banker," she said as she nodded toward a small window in the far corner that was sealed off by a heavy iron grate. "I can pick up your thousand right now. Just wait here."

"On second thought," Slocum said as he picked out a few of Theil's men from the crowd milling between the tables, "you should probably just get your chips and settle into a game. I'll come by to collect my fee in a bit."

"All right." Eliza kissed Slocum on the cheek and practically skipped away like a little girl going to her first day of school.

Although Slocum watched her cross the room and head over to the banker's cage, he was more interested in the men that were watching her. Some of those fellows were of the normal variety and were mostly interested in the shift of her hips beneath her skirts or the bounce of her perky breasts. The others were the ones that concerned Slocum the most. Most of them were on Armand Theil's payroll.

Not until Slocum started winding his way through the crowd was he so glad that Eliza had insisted upon him buying that new suit. Most of the gamblers that had found their way to the Straight Deal were dressed in a similar fashion, right down to the dark coat and watch chain crossing their midsections. All Slocum had to do was keep his head low and his hat pulled down a ways for him to blend in nicely.

As he got closer to the busiest batch of tables toward the back of the room, Slocum could feel the excitement in the air. Each game had a sense of grandness to it that was centered around all the money piled in front of each player. The gamblers were well dressed and glancing about at the other players as well as the other tables. Servers carried drinks and working girls made their rounds, tying all the tables into a whole.

With the brim of his hat coming down low over his eyes, Slocum wasn't able to see as much as he would have liked. He made that sacrifice willingly since most of his face was covered up along the way. With plenty of men sidling back and forth trying to keep from being noticed, Slocum figured he wouldn't have any trouble getting swallowed up by this crowd. Judging by the surprised expression on Lem's face, he was right.

"Where have you been?" Slocum asked as he crept up to Lem's side.

Obviously doing his best to watch the crowd through his cracked spectacles, Lem growled, "You got me confused for someone else."

Slocum lifted his chin and used one finger to push up the brim of his hat just enough for Lem to get a look at his face. "I don't think so."

Upon recognizing Slocum, Lem pulled in half a breath and snapped his hand down toward his hip.

Since Lem hadn't been involved in the earlier scuffle, Slocum guessed there was a good chance he could have escaped the ire of the Straight Deal's guards. Sure enough, Lem had either been overlooked when Theil and his men were banned from carrying firearms in the place, or Lem had snuck one in on his own. Rather than take the time to figure out which of those had occurred, Slocum snapped his hand toward Lem's holster with the same speed he would use to clear leather on his own.

Actually, since Slocum wasn't worried about finding a trigger and aiming afterward, his speed was just a little better than normal. In the blink of an eye, Slocum had plucked out Lem's gun and claimed it for himself.

Lem kept slapping at his holster even after he'd already realized it was empty. His eyes were wide as saucers and his mouth gaped like a fish that had been tossed onto the bottom of a boat. "Where . . . where the hell did you come from?"

Jabbing Lem with the barrel of his own gun, Slocum said, "I came from Hell, asshole. Now I can send you back in my place."

To say that Lem panicked would have been an understatement.

Under most circumstances, the sight of the skinny fellow reeling from Slocum and scampering away as if the sky was falling would have been funny. Slocum somehow managed to keep from smirking while he also kept the fire in his eyes and the gun in his hand.

After bouncing against some other gamblers and knocking over a server carrying a tray full of drinks, Lem lost his footing and stumbled toward the bar. Sid was tending that stretch of the long bar, and he rushed forward to get to Lem before anything valuable was broken.

"Had a little too much to drink tonight, sir?" Sid asked.

Lem stared across the bar at Sid. The cracks in his spectacles made his eyeballs appear splintered and distorted. "There's a man over there with a gun," he said.

"Lost of folks carry guns, sir, but don't fret about it. Our own boys keep a real good eye on things."

"That ain't what I mean, damn you! That man took *my* gun and means to take a shot at me! He would'a killed me if I didn't get away from him. Now if you and your boys are putting Mr. Theil on notice, why the hell does that asshole get to roam around and do what he pleases?"

Like any good barkeep dealing with a babbling fool, Sid calmly stood and waited for Lem to finish. When Lem was done spouting, Sid leaned to one side so he could glance past him. "What man are you talking about, sir?"

"That one," Lem snapped as he wheeled around to point out Slocum. He wasn't too surprised that Slocum wasn't exactly where he'd left him, but Lem was taken aback when he couldn't spot Slocum at all. Even with his cracked spectacles, Lem should have been able to spot a prairie dog sticking his head up at fifty yards. It's what he got paid to do. This time, however, his prairie dog had up and disappeared. "He was right there! He had a black hat and coat. Gray pants! Find him, goddammit!"

"Black hat and coat, huh?" Sid asked as he looked around to find at least a couple dozen men that matched that description. "I'll be sure to keep my eyes open."

Lem jumped across the bar with enough speed to rule him out as just another drunk. Before Sid could reach for any of the weapons stashed under his bar, Lem had grabbed hold of the front of his shirt and pulled him forward.

"We paid for protection here, smart-ass," Lem snarled. "We followed your rules. Do your fucking job and find that prick. His name's John Slocum!"

"Unhand me, sir."

"The hell I—"

Lem was cut short as a massive paw slammed down upon his shoulder and closed tight enough to cut off the blood through that entire arm. When he brought his elbow back, it thumped uselessly against a solid wall of muscle.

"Should I hurt him, Sid?" Grizzly asked.

Sid straightened his shirt and asked, "I don't know. Is he willing to behave?"

Lem knew when he was beat and he hung from Grizzly's hand like a kitten dangling by the scruff of its neck. "I just want to let you know Slocum is breaking the rules. He's got a gun and means to use it."

"All right, then. You know who Slocum is?" Sid asked.

Grizzly nodded. "I already searched him."

"Then see if you can find him and make sure he's staying in line. We don't want anyone causing a ruckus when we've got such a full house. That do, sir?"

Lem nodded to the barkeep and did a bit of posturing to reclaim some of his dignity. Pushing his broken spectacles up along his nose, Lem replied, "It's all I ask. If I find him again, I'll be sure to—"

"You won't do shit," Grizzly said. "I've heard more'n enough out of you."

"All right," Lem sputtered. "Fine. I'll be on my way." When he tried to walk away, he was stopped and roughly patted down.

Grizzly plucked a pair of knives and a backup pistol from Lem's pockets and boots. Handing the weapons over to the barkeep, he snarled, "Now you can go."

Although Lem muttered a few obscenities as he walked away, he made certain to keep his voice low enough to keep from being heard.

"You really want me to find this fella he was howling about?" Grizzly asked.

After about two seconds of consideration, Sid shook his head. "The boss pointed out this John Slocum fella to me after that killing in the back. I met him earlier and he was an amicable enough sort. I'll have a word with him if I spot him. Are you concerned about him?"

"Nah."

"Then you just be sure to keep an eye on that rat with the eyeglasses."

Grizzly nodded and moved away from the bar.

Sid grinned and went back to pouring firewater. He sincerely hoped Lem would stay in line. The last thing Sid wanted was to clean up that mess.

17

Eliza hadn't sat down at Theil's table right away. She'd started at one of the first tables she could find where she recognized most of the other players. Since she'd already wrapped those men around her finger at various times at various saloons in several towns, getting them hooked again wasn't too difficult. Her dress hugged her curves nicely and had a bodice that was laced up the front, which made it that much easier to loosen so her natural assets could be seen a little better.

When she'd sat down at the table, she'd smiled and patted the men's hands in the way she knew they liked. When she raked in her winnings, she leaned forward to give them all a nice consolation prize, and when she lost, she pouted while coyly playing with her hair. To her credit, Eliza was doing a lot more of the former than the latter.

"It sure is good to see you again, Eliza," a man by the name of Steve said as he glanced down the front of her dress.

Although the pot wasn't as big as most of the others she'd won, Eliza leaned forward a bit more to bring it in. Her breasts were barely contained by her loosely fitted top, and she lingered for a few moments before sitting back and wagging a finger at Steve. "Naughty boy. You should pay more attention to your game."

"I'd rather pay attention to yours."

"We'll just have to wait and see what we can do about that."

The man to Eliza's left had the cards and was shuffling them for the next round. He was an older fellow with skin that was just a bit too loose for his face, and took in an eyeful of Eliza, but managed to shake himself free a little sooner than the younger gents at the table. "Right now we're still playin'. That is, unless you want to excuse yourselves."

"I like it here," Eliza purred. "I'm feeling lucky."

Steve started to reply to that, but cut himself off and shifted his eyes to a spot behind her chair. "You admiring the view, mister?"

Slocum stepped up to Eliza and looked down. "Actually, I am."

"Well, ante up and play or step aside," the older fellow said. "This ain't a stage show."

Waving off the older man's gaze, Eliza scooted back from the table and said, "I think I'll stretch my legs. If you'll excuse me, gentlemen." She ignored the protests from Steve and the others while organizing her winnings so she could pick them up and carry them away.

Helping her by taking some of the stacks of chips, Slocum led her through the maze of tables and whispered, "I found Theil. He's playing at a table right over there."

"I know where he's at, silly," Eliza said. "I just needed to build up my funds."

"Seems like you've done that well enough."

"I have. I was ready to move over to Theil as soon as you cleared the way. Did you find his men?"

"Oh, yeah," Slocum replied with a chuckle. "After I found Lem, the rest were just as easy. In fact, Lem made a big enough ass out of himself that he got the guards in this poker hall watching them better than I could. Dawes was easy enough to spot. A big man that squawks that much when he's hurt doesn't have any business trying to sneak about."

"Perfect."

"So, do you think you're ready to take Theil to the cleaners?"

"I've been ready for a long time," Eliza said with a confident sparkle in her eyes. "Why do you think that bastard didn't even want me to get here?"

"Good. Let's get you to his table so you can . . ." When he felt the familiar touch of Eliza's arm snaking around his own, Slocum stopped talking and looked over at her. What caught his attention the most was the fact that she was purposely leading him away from the poker tables. "What are you doing?" he asked.

"I can't have you escort me directly to the table," she said. "You're doing your best work keeping out of sight. What happened to your hat?"

Thrown off by the sudden change of subject, Slocum reached up to tap the brim of the dark gray bowler that sat atop his head. "Oh, I've been swapping hats with a few drunks here and there. It keeps me from getting picked out of the crowd too easily. You were right about this suit. Damn near everyone in this place is wearing one just like it."

Eliza had made it to one of the walls in the room that wasn't taken up by the bar. She pushed open a door marked "Private" and pulled Slocum inside. "And you look damn good in it, too," she purred.

As far as Slocum could tell, the door opened to a narrow room used to store cleaning supplies. The noise from the main room was enough to rattle the walls around them and nobody was interested in following them into the long, narrow closet. "What the hell are we doing in here?" Slocum asked.

Already tugging at Slocum's belt buckle, Eliza said, "Celebrating. I've already won more than enough to stake my run against Theil with a sweet little profit besides."

Slocum stepped up to pin Eliza to the wall while also

savoring the way she squirmed against him. "You've got my advance?"

"It's in my pocket," she said while guiding his hand along the side of her skirt. "Come and get it."

Reaching into her skirt, Slocum found a pocket that was sewn into her skirt and ran all the way down to the middle of her thigh. It was deep enough to carry several rolls of money and a little knife to boot. Slocum eased his hand past the money and rubbed the curve of her thigh through the soft material. She let out an anxious breath as he reached around to grab her backside while still keeping his hand in her hidden pocket. The moment he cupped her tight little ass, Slocum felt Eliza's leg come up to rub against his own.

"That's right, John. Come and get it."

Slocum nearly ripped her dress apart as he took his hand from her pocket. A few of the items hidden in there hit the floor as he gathered up her skirts and bunched them around her waist to find she wasn't wearing any clothing under them. Eliza set her leg down so she could pull Slocum's jeans down, and once she'd freed his rigid cock, she wrapped her leg around him again. Slocum was quick to grab her ass with both hands and lift her up so she could wrap both her legs around him and lock her ankles against the small of his back.

Enjoying the feel of Eliza's tight backside in his hands, Slocum moved her around until he felt the tip of his erection brush against the wet lips of her pussy. Once there, he buried his cock into the soft tangle of hair between her legs and slammed her against the wall.

Eliza tightened her grip, closed her eyes, and arched her back. She moved her hips in time to Slocum's rhythm as he pumped in and out of her. Eliza's shoulders hit the wall again and again, but she didn't make enough noise to trump the noise that was coming from the main room.

"God, yes, John. Do it harder."

Slocum was more than willing to oblige. He pounded into her a few more times before someone knocked at the door to his immediate left. When he heard that, he froze like a deer in a hunter's sights.

"Someone in there?" asked a muffled voice on the other side of the door.

Reaching over to grab the door handle, Slocum was able to hold it in place as the person on the other side tried to get it open. After a few tries, the person gave up and walked away.

The blood was still rushing through Slocum's veins and, judging by the way her chest heaved, Eliza was feeling much the same way. She stood leaning back against the wall, waiting impatiently for Slocum to turn his attention back to her. Once Slocum saw the hungry look in her eyes, he grabbed Eliza by the back of the head and pulled her in for a strong kiss.

Their mouths pressed against each other and her tongue slipped past his lips. When Slocum came up for some air, he spun her around so she was facing the wall, lifted her skirts, and grabbed hold of her bare hips. Eliza pressed both palms against the wall and stuck her backside out for him. In a matter of seconds, Slocum had entered her from behind.

Slocum's hard cock slipped easily in and out of Eliza's dripping pussy. As if the feel of her wasn't enough, the sight of her tight, round little ass wiggling every time he pounded into her nearly drove him over the edge.

"You like that?" Slocum asked, even though he already knew the answer.

Eliza's reply was a fierce whisper. "Just don't stop," she said as she held her skirts up with one hand and used the other to brace herself against the wall.

Keeping his knees bent, Slocum was able to slide up into her at just the right angle. When he pumped forward, he pulled her back until their bodies met. Slocum hit his stride and pumped in and out of her, faster and faster, like a train that picked up speed as it rolled downhill.

He felt Eliza start to tremble, so Slocum reached around to rub his finger along the tender nub of her clit. That caused her to yelp in surprise as an orgasm shot through her like wildfire. Eliza managed to bite down on her lip before making too much noise, but her restraint was put to the test as Slocum thrust even harder between her legs.

A few more strokes, and Slocum felt his entire body start to ache for release. He didn't hold back one second before grabbing her ass tightly and holding her steady as he gave her one last powerful thrust. The moment her ass bumped against him, Slocum exploded inside her.

He stayed put for a few seconds, admiring the feel of Elisa's smooth skin against the palms of his hands. Before too long, however, the rush of blood faded from his ears and the sounds from the rest of the saloon made themselves known to him.

"You wait right here," Eliza said breathlessly as she disengaged from him and straightened her skirts. "Give me a minute or two to announce myself to Theil and then you can do your part. You think you can keep his boys away from that table?"

"That job's already mostly done. What about my advance?"

Eliza smirked as she dropped to one knee and collected some of the things that had fallen from her pocket. When she spoke again, she opened her lips wide as if she meant to start in on him all over again from her knees. "Here you go," she said as she handed him one of the bundles of cash. "You've earned it."

Putting the money into his pocket, Slocum watched Eliza slip out the door and into the main room. He could tell she'd found it amusing to be the one paying him after what had just happened, but Slocum let her have her little joke. As long as she pulled her weight in this partnership, she could have all the fun she wanted. From where Slocum was standing, there was more than enough benefit to keep their arrangement going.

Unlike the first time Slocum had walked into the Straight Deal, he had no trouble picking Eliza out of the crowd. Every table in the place may have been occupied and there may have been plenty of gamblers milling among them, but the main event was difficult to miss. Eliza and Theil sat across from each other with four other players in the game with them. Every time Slocum glanced over at that table throughout the night, the pile of money in the middle of it just kept growing.

As much as Slocum would have liked to watch the game more closely or even sit in on it, he had a job to do that didn't have a thing to do with playing cards. Theil's men were easy enough to spot. The hired guns were on their guard after the cat-and-mouse game that had played earlier. Fortunately, now was the time when Slocum didn't mind being seen.

As the hours wore on and card after card was dealt, Theil's men kept testing how close they could get to the table before Slocum could get in front of them. It was getting close to the time when late night would become early morning, and the latest one to try their luck was Dawes. Slocum spotted the big man easily enough and made his way over to stand next to him.

"Don't you ever sleep?" Dawes grumbled.

Glancing down at the cane in the big man's hand, Slocum replied, "Haven't you ever heard of a doctor?"

"The bullet just cut through the meat," Dawes said as he shifted uncomfortably off the leg with the wounded shin.

"What about your arm?"

Dawes winced and shifted the arm that had been run through with Andy's blade. It was kept in a sling that hung beneath his coat. "I had worse. Besides, it ain't like any of us can get close to that table anyhow. See for yerself."

Slocum spotted another pair of Theil's men. Lem walked beside another fellow who wore an empty double-rig holster around his waist. Before either man could get within ten feet of the table where Eliza and Theil were playing, two of the Straight Deal's own men stepped up and cleared their throats to announce their presence. Lem and the other man promptly stepped away.

"That one with the double rig was in the back room," Slocum pointed out. "Who is he?"

"That's Edmonson," Dawes announced.

"Should that impress me?"

"I thought you might have heard of him. He's killed plenty of gunfighters like you."

Slocum shrugged and looked around for a second before he spotted Mark sneaking toward the table. Upon seeing that, he caught Grizzly's eye and pointed Mark out. "You boys can't be stupid enough to try anything while that game's going on. You've got to know none of you would make it out alive. Considering how hot under the collar the owner of this place got with that last bit of trouble, I doubt he'd let your boss walk out of here with any of his money if he stirred up more trouble. Either that, or the owner would lock Theil up and take the money back for court fees."

"I know," Dawes sighed. "We got our orders."

When Slocum looked at the big man, he almost felt sorry for him. Dawes leaned against the cane using his one good arm to nurse a wounded leg and support the weight of an empty holster strapped around his waist. Even the big man's eyes were dim as lanterns sputtering on their last bit of fuel.

"You don't have to do this, you know," Slocum said.

"Huh?"

"You men don't have guns. It's almost dawn and you haven't even been able to get close enough to have a word with your boss."

"We've spoken," Dawes said.

Nodding, Slocum replied, "Oh, right. Whenever Theil heads to the shithouse, you or the others must have a little meeting. I'll bet these doormen barely even give you any privacy in there." Seeing the pathetic twitch in the corner of Dawes's eye told Slocum that he was on the right path. "You've all been walking down to some other shithouse to meet, haven't you?"

"None of yer concern," Dawes snapped.

Slocum looked at the table where Eliza was leaning down to rake in another pot. She had to spread her arms open wide and lean forward to gather all the chips and cash. When she spotted Slocum, she winked and blew him a little kiss.

"Sure looks like Theil's in the shithouse to me," Slocum said. "Only one other player besides him is sticking around to keep getting whipped."

Sure enough, there was only one other man at the table with Eliza and Theil. From what Slocum had learned during the course of the night, that man was a cattle baron who was tossing around fortunes as just another way to amuse himself for a night. The cattle baron was down to a short stack of chips, but he seemed to be willing to stay as long as Eliza kept her buttons open far enough to give him a show when she won. Slocum had to shake his head at how consistently that simple trick worked.

"Theil's on his last legs," Slocum said. "Anyone with a set of eyes can see that. Whatever he's paying you, he won't be able to pony up when he's done getting cleaned out like this."

"We'll see about that, Slocum."

"Maybe. Or maybe you and the rest of his hired guns are doing a night's work for free. What good is it to work for a man who can't afford to pay?"

Dawes grumbled under his breath and shifted once more upon his wounded leg.

"Are you willing to die on the off chance that Theil can get lucky enough to beat her? I mean, he doesn't strike me as the sort who would hold aside your fee to make sure he didn't gamble it away, so that means you and your men will only keep getting paid if he beats her. Do you even think he *can* beat her? If he could, wouldn't he have been willing to let her get to this game in one piece?"

Before Dawes could answer any of those questions, a loud crash brought everyone's attention to Eliza and Theil's table. That crash came from Theil's fist slamming against the felt-covered wood.

"Cheating bitch!" Theil shouted.

Eliza leaned back and looked at him with wide eyes. "A straight flush beats four of a kind. Hasn't that always been the case, Armand?"

"How'd you get that straight flush?"

Eliza batted her eyelashes and said, "I'm just lucky, I suppose."

"Lucky?" Theil fumed. "Nobody's that fucking lucky! I suppose it was fucking luck that let you beat me those other times?"

"Not hardly," Eliza said. "Most of the times I was just plain better than you."

A hush fell upon that entire section of the room as if everyone there could feel how Eliza's words grated against Theil's ears. When Theil hissed his next words, everyone in the vicinity could hear him.

"You're dead, bitch. I'll tan your cheating hide and beat that smug fucking grin off that pretty little face."

Slocum rushed toward the table and was prepared to push aside anyone that got in his way. Theil's men started to make their move, but the Straight Deal's guards rushed forward to keep them in check. Once she saw she had the protection of all those men around her, Eliza said, "I think I want to leave now. Could I please have these chips cashed out?"

The owner of the Straight Deal was a tall man in a suit that would have been perfectly at home wrapped around an undertaker. The few times Slocum had seen him, the owner's hands had been clasped behind his back. This time was no exception.

"Cash her out," the owner said. "Then it's probably best if she is escorted out."

"Fine with me," Eliza said.

Slocum stayed with her in the minute or so it took for her money to be brought to her. "Do you know how much I won, John?" she asked in an excited whisper.

"That can wait. Let's just get the hell out of here."

"Why? Are Theil's men coming?"

"No. They're already gone."

18

Slocum may have escorted Eliza out of the Straight Deal without any trouble, but he wasn't happy. Eliza may have won a boatload of money, which she'd promised to cut him in on, but Slocum still wasn't happy. Theil had disappeared along with all of his men and there were only a few possibilities as to where they could have gone.

"Maybe they went to lick their wounds or leave town," Eliza offered.

"Or they're waiting for us," Slocum said, giving voice to the last of the possibilities. All he and Eliza needed to do was leave the Straight Deal and round the corner for them to find out which of the possibilities was correct.

This was one of the times Slocum would have been perfectly happy if he'd been wrong.

Mark stepped from the boardwalk and onto the street. Dawes remained in his spot on the other side of the street. Edmonson leaned against a post no more than twelve paces away from Slocum, which meant Lem had to be lurking about somewhere.

The door to a small restaurant a bit farther down the street opened and two men stepped outside. "I want my money, Banner!" Theil said as he walked out of The Cooking Fire.

Eliza lifted her chin, and would have stormed toward Theil if Slocum hadn't grabbed her arm and pulled her back. "I won that money," she declared. "You played a hell of a game, but I won. If you hadn't thrown such a fit, you might have gotten a chance to win it back."

"I did play a hell of a game. You just cheated a hell of a lot more."

"Prove it!"

Theil stood perched at the edge of the boardwalk, staring daggers across the street at Eliza. The man next to him had his hand resting on the top of his holster in a way that made it obvious that holster was no longer empty. In fact, as Slocum took a look around at the rest of the men, he could see every one of them had rearmed themselves after leaving the Straight Deal.

Shaking his head, Theil said, "If I could prove it, I would have."

"And if you could have beat me, you would have," Eliza shot back. "Remember that game in Denver? You tried palming that queen and playing it two hands later. You can't even swindle me, Armand. No wonder you wanted me dead."

"Well, I suppose some things don't change."

Slocum didn't like the sound of that. The moment he saw Theil nod toward the gunmen lining the street, he pulled Eliza back so she was behind him. A half second later, Edmonson pulled one of the guns from his double rig and got the party started.

If Slocum hadn't needed to hide one of the guns he'd stolen during the night, he could have reached it quickly enough to beat Edmonson to the punch. As it was, Slocum drew the gun he'd tucked at the small of his back and fired at the same time as Edmonson. Slocum stood his ground and Edmonson flinched as a bullet whipped less than an inch from his temple.

Knowing his shot wasn't a killing blow as soon as he'd pulled the trigger, Slocum took advantage of the time his near miss had bought him. "Get behind me and keep your head down," he said as he tossed Eliza toward a nearby water trough.

As soon as she hit the ground, Eliza curled up into a ball and covered her head with both arms.

In the space of a heartbeat, Slocum had seen enough to tell him which of the other gunmen he needed to worry about. They had all drawn their weapons, but only Edmonson and Dawes held their ground. Mark fired a few quick shots to cover himself as he dove behind a barrel, and the gunman closest to Theil ran toward Slocum while gripping a pistol in each hand. Although he unleashed a thunderous round of fire from those guns, his shots were wild, and only became wilder as the recoil started building up.

"Now—Lem!" Mark shouted into the air. "Now, goddammit!"

Slocum followed Mark's line of sight and spotted Lem poking his head up from the top of The Cooking Fire. Extending his arm to point in that direction, Slocum fired three quick shots at the rooftop. He wasn't sure he'd hit Lem, but he'd done enough to convince Lem to stay down for a little while longer.

"Move up!" Edmonson hollered.

It wasn't much of a rallying cry, but it was enough to get most of the gunmen walking toward Slocum and Eliza. Edmonson fired a shot from one gun while keeping his other in its holster for when it was needed. The second two-gun shooter wasn't so organized. He screwed up another batch of courage and ran at Slocum with both guns blazing.

Not willing to gamble on all those shots missing, Slocum dropped to one knee and fired at the wild kid with the twin pistols. That shot was pulled off its course thanks to a stray round that clipped Slocum's sleeve. Slocum's next shot felt good the moment he fired it, but the one after that felt even better. The two-gun shooter stopped as if he'd hit a brick wall, and then fell back with blood spraying from his chest.

Slocum tossed the empty gun away and pulled the other six-shooter he'd been hiding under his coat. This was the gun he'd stolen from Lem, so it was only fitting that Lem caught the first round from it. Upon seeing Lem peek up from the top of The Cooking Fire, Slocum shot as if he was going for the smallest target in a shooting gallery. Lem ducked, but didn't fall.

The gunmen sent more shots Slocum's way as they grew accustomed to being under fire. Mark fired off a shot that scratched Slocum's side. Edmonson was working his way along the side of the street to get closer to him, but Dawes worried Slocum the most simply because he was taking the time to sight along the gun's barrel.

Slocum fired a shot that was a little low and to one side. It must have been Dawes's lucky day because Slocum's shot was on target and knocked the cane right out from under him. Dawes toppled over and landed on his wounded leg, swore up a storm, and then rolled onto his wounded arm.

Slocum hustled toward the water trough where Eliza was still taking cover.

"Behind you!" she shouted.

Slocum dropped his right shoulder down as he allowed his own momentum to carry him toward the ground. Tucking his body in, Slocum was able to hit the ground on his arm, roll until he was facing Theil's men, and then take a moment to see what danger Eliza had warned him about. The only thing he could see from that angle was The Cooking Fire. With the sky just starting to be smeared by the first hints of dawn, Slocum was also able to see Lem lining up a shot from his spot on the roof.

Aiming from instinct more than anything else, Slocum fired a shot that punched through the upper portion of the restaurant's sign. Fortunately, Lem had been hiding behind that very sign, and he straightened up when he caught a chunk of hot lead in the belly. The pistol in Slocum's hand barked again, spitting out a shot that punched through the middle of Lem's face.

Lem wavered for a second before falling back and hitting the roof with a resounding thump.

"Are you all right?" Slocum asked when he finally got to Eliza's side. "Are you hit?"

She shook her head quickly. "No. You?"

"Ask me again in a few minutes." With that, Slocum took a tentative look around the water trough.

The street was clear. Theil stood in the doorway of the restaurant so he could duck back in at any time. His remaining gunmen were scattered on either side of the street. Dawes was the only one of those that Slocum could pick out right away, since the big man was still rolling on the boardwalk and cursing in pain. Now that the gunshots had faded, Slocum could hear other voices nearby. He turned to look, and found several locals and gamblers lining the street behind him as if they were fighting to get a better look at a boxing match.

Grizzly stood among those people like a single oak planted in a field of weeds. He looked right back at Slocum and then casually pointed to Slocum's left. Slocum turned in that direction, but was too late to stop Edmonson as he rushed toward Eliza.

"Son of a bitch!" Slocum grunted as he swung his gun around to get a shot off. By the time his gun was pointed in the right direction, Slocum's biggest target was Eliza herself.

Edmonson crouched directly behind Eliza with his gun's barrel pressed against her head. "Go on, killer," he taunted. "Take a shot at me and hope I don't twitch on this trigger."

Slocum figured up his odds on dropping Edmonson without Eliza getting hurt, and they weren't good. He lowered his gun and let out a haggard breath.

"That's what I thought," Edmonson said. "Now stand up, darlin'."

Eliza stood up and Edmonson stayed right behind her. He wrapped one arm across her front to drag her toward The Cooking Fire, but quickly shifted his grip so he could grope her breasts. "Stop it!" she screamed.

"I'm more than willing to let this matter come to an end," Theil said once he finally stepped out of the restaurant. "Just admit you cheated me and give me back my money."

"This has already gone way past that," Slocum said.

Theil looked over at him and nodded. "It sure has, but that's your fault."

"Your men started the shooting. That's why I got dragged into this in the first place!"

"Fine. Edmonson, just take my damned money. She must have it hidden on her somewhere."

"With pleasure," Edmonson sneered. "If that killer drops that smoke wagon of his, I might just let this little lady squirm while I go looking. Otherways, I could just take it from her after she hits the ground."

That was the card that Slocum had hoped wouldn't be played. At least, he'd hoped he could let enough time pass that Edmonson would get too comfortable and give him a clearer shot or do something to encourage someone else to step in and put an end to the fight. Unfortunately, Edmonson was still hiding behind Eliza, and everyone else in the vicinity seemed perfectly content to watch.

"Come on now," Edmonson snarled. "This bitch is pretty, but I ain't opposed to opening her up for everyone to see."

Eliza's struggling tapered off as she felt the gun barrel press even harder against her head. With no more brave words to spout, she closed her eyes and tried not to cry.

Taking one last look to see if Eliza had any admirers willing to step up and be counted, Slocum spotted Grizzly on the side of the street no more than five yards away from him. The big man wasn't making a direct move against Theil or his remaining gunmen, but gave Slocum a brief glimpse at something even better.

"I drop the gun and he lets her go," Slocum said. "Then she can hand back the money."

Theil had not only left the safety of his own place, but he and Mark were strolling toward Slocum as if they didn't have a care in the world. When he spoke, Theil seemed to be addressing the crowd rather than talking to Slocum or Eliza. "If that will prevent more bloodshed, then I agree. I am, after all, a peaceful man."

"Peaceful men don't hire gunhands to chase a lady from one town to another while shooting at her every step of the way," Slocum pointed out. "And they don't attack her when the odds are five to one against that same lady."

"Drop the gun or we'll kill you both right now," Theil said as he drew his own nickel-plated .45 from under his coat. "I'm sick of dealing with the both of you."

Grizzly stood nearby, right where he'd been the last time Slocum had checked. The big man even nodded once as if to encourage Slocum to keep his wits about him. If Slocum had had more than two bullets left in his cylinder, he might have acted a whole lot differently. But since there were currently more targets than bullets, Slocum opened his fingers and let his gun drop from his hand. It fell to the ground and came to rest against his boot.

"Kick it away," Edmonson said.

Slocum kicked the gun away.

"Good," Theil shouted. "Now show Mr. Slocum and everyone here what happens to cheaters."

Edmonson's face split into a wicked smile as he tightened his grip on his gun and grabbed Eliza by the back of her neck.

"Slocum!" Grizzly bellowed from his spot on the boardwalk.

Slocum turned toward Grizzly. The big man was still nearby and was still holding the Colt Navy he'd shown Slocum a few seconds ago. Grizzly tossed the six-shooter so Slocum could snatch it from the air.

"Eliza!" Slocum hollered as his own Colt was finally returned to him. "Duck!"

Edmonson's smile quickly turned into a pained grimace as Eliza stomped his foot beneath her heel and dropped to her knees.

The first shot Slocum fired went over Eliza's head, but was too rushed to hit its mark. The bullet came close enough to rattle Edmonson and loosen his grip, which allowed Eliza to pull away from him. When Slocum fired his next round, he knew it was a good one.

Edmonson wheeled around on one foot and sent his gun sailing across the street. He dropped to one knee, let out a gurgling breath, and drew the second pistol from his double-rig holster.

Slocum's Colt barked a third time and sent a round hissing through the air like an angry hornet to punch a third eye through Edmonson's skull. Shifting his attention to Mark and Theil, Slocum glared at them over the top of his gun and spoke one word.

"Don't."

After seeing the other men fall, and knowing Slocum had enough rounds in his gun to finish the job, both Theil and Mark lowered their hands and carefully placed their pistols on the ground.

"Is there a jail in this damned town?" Slocum asked.

Grizzly led a few others from the crowd to step in and grab hold of Theil and Mark. "But she cheated me!" Theil insisted. Fixing his eyes on Grizzly, he added, "Your boss knows better than anyone what happens to cheaters around here!"

"Sure," Grizzly said. "Now let me show you what happens to sniveling pricks who try to kill a woman in the middle of the street."

As Theil and Mark were led away by a crowd that grew more unruly by the second, Slocum holstered his Colt and walked over to Eliza. "You all right?" he asked after helping her up.

Her cheeks were flushed and some tear tracks ran from her eyes, but she cleaned herself off and nodded. "I'm fine. Thanks to you."

"If you want to thank me, how about paying me my cut?"

She smiled and dug both of her hands deep into the pockets that were sewn into the sides of her skirts. When she took her hands out again, they were filled with money.

Slocum wrapped his arm around her and turned Eliza away from the crowd. "All right, all right. You made your point. Put that away while we've still got a chance of leaving this town with it. How much is there?"

"Sixty-eight thousand, four hundred dollars."

"Damn. So my portion is—"

"That is your portion, John," Eliza whispered excitedly. "And you earned every last cent of it." Seeing the look on Slocum's face, Eliza nodded and showed him her devilish grin. "I told you I could clean him out. I also put a dent into some of those other rich fellows at that table along the way."

"Then perhaps all of this was worth the trouble," Slocum said. "Let me just ask you one thing. Did you cheat?"

"Hell, yes, I cheated. I used every trick in the book. Since Theil ran me out of all those towns, hired those dogs to scare me every moment I played, and tried to kill us both more times than I can recall, I figure he deserved to lose his money one way or another."

Slocum shook his head. "And he still couldn't catch you red-handed or prove what you did?"

"He sure couldn't," Eliza replied with genuine disbelief. "I guess I really am lucky."

Watch for

SLOCUM AND THE WITCH OF WESTLAKE

362nd novel in the exciting SLOCUM series
from Jove

Coming in April!

DON'T MISS A YEAR OF

Slocum Giant
by
Jake Logan

Slocum Giant 2004:
Slocum in the Secret Service

Slocum Giant 2005:
Slocum and the Larcenous Lady

Slocum Giant 2006:
Slocum and the Hanging Horse

Slocum Giant 2007:
Slocum and the Celestial Bones

Slocum Giant 2008:
Slocum and the Town Killers

penguin.com/actionwesterns